Exit Laughing

Come and trip it as you go
You are going to die, you know,
Willy-nilly fall in line
And be in death my valentine
                                    Lucy

This poison-pen doggerel brought along Hildegarde Withers to investigate what was going on in that section of the Miracle-Paradox film studios where the cartoons featuring 'Peter Penguin' were made. On her way to report for her first day's work in the studio, Hildegarde found a corpse; someone had fed Larry Reed, a cartoon artist, with a very lethal dose of poison-ivy. Hildegarde was quite capable of taking a murder in her maidenly stride, but her erstwhile collaborator, Inspector Oscar Piper, felt sure the old girl was getting out of her depth: he flew into Los Angeles from New York to help her.

And sure enough there were more poison pens and more poison-ivy before the undaunted Hildegarde unveiled the murderer of Miracle-Paradox in as sensational a climax as Stuart Palmer ever fashioned for her.

This title was first published in the Crime Club in 1954.

STUART PALMER

Exit Laughing

Hildegarde Withers investigates ...

The Disappearing Detectives
*Selected and Introduced
by H. R. F. Keating*

COLLINS, 8 GRAFTON STREET, LONDON W1

William Collins Sons & Co. Ltd
London · Glasgow · Sydney · Auckland
Toronto · Johannesburg

First published in the Crime Club 1954
Reprinted in this edition 1985
Copyright reserved Stuart Palmer
© in the Introduction, H. R. F. Keating, 1985

British Library Cataloguing in Publication Data

Palmer, Stuart
    Exit Laughing.—(Disappearing detectives).—
(Crime Club)
    I. Title   II. Series
    823'.912[F]   PR6031.A38/

    ISBN 0 00 231424 X

Photoset in Linotron Baskerville by
Rowland Phototypesetting Ltd
Bury St Edmunds, Suffolk
Printed in Great Britain by
William Collins Sons & Co. Ltd, Glasgow

To WALTER LANTZ, the creator of the illimitable Woody Woodpecker (who appears here slightly disguised) in gratitude for his friendly cooperation. And to TED SEARS, of the Walt Disney Studios, for his invaluable assistance. Long may they wave.

—S.P.

INTRODUCTION
H. R. F. Keating

Odd to reflect that of the dozen fictional detectives I have attempted in this series to prevent disappearing entirely from readers' view Stuart Palmer's Hildegarde Withers, Hildy, is at the same time the one least in need of such assistance and by and large the one least deserving of it. Hildegarde is still clearly with us, if only just. As recently as August 1984 she appeared on some TV screens in a pilot film (which sank) called *A Very Missing Person*, in which she was portrayed, somewhat smartened up from the original conception, by Eve Arden. Indeed, since Hildegarde appeared in six films made from the books, notably starring the correctly horse-faced Edna May Oliver, it is not impossible that she will be a late, late movie for years to come.

She was, too, I find, the only one of my present chosen twelve whom I also picked out in 1983 as one of some 90 'People of Crime' in an encyclopædia I edited called *Whodunit*. Yet really in many ways she does not deserve quite this pre-eminence. Hildegarde Withers is, frankly, no more than a cartoon figure, though as striking a one as . . . 'Peter Penguin', the co-hero of this book set appropriately in the world of Hollywood cartoon-making.

Conceived originally as a schoolmarm sleuth from a tough New York school, she was equipped with a rag-bag clutch of possibly useful characteristics: her apricot poodle Talleyrand, a series of outrageous hats, a love for fish-tanks and their denizens (dropped when her creator, having moved to California, gave her some hasty asthma and swept her across the continent in his wake). But she was never allowed more depth than a penny piece.

She was, however, based on a real person, or rather on

two. First, Mr Palmer once admitted, she was his high schoolteacher, Miss Fern Hackett, and second she was his father. From them perhaps she got her two most uncartoon-like qualities, her unquashable tendency to poke her nose into things ('I like to meddle,' she says in this book) and her impatience with stupidity. It was the latter, perversely endearing quality that launched her on her career in *The Penguin Pool Murder* in 1931 and gave her creator with its success both as book and film a lifelong fascination with penguins that culminated in 1954 in this book (called *Cold Poison* in the US), the one but last to feature Hildegarde. In 1931, taking her class to a New York aquarium and finding a body in the penguin pool, she became so exasperated with police stupidity that she launched into investigation herself.

It was a not too unlikely thing, and a schoolteacher makes a not too improbable figure as a successful amateur sleuth. A person whose profession it is to sum up the characters of some 30 or 40 young human beings, to keep a sharp eye open to circumvent their inherent tendency to mischief of all sorts, has acquired already the essentials for sorting out murder riddles. This is a fact that has struck other writers than Stuart Palmer. Alice Tilton's retired schoolmaster, Leonidas Witherall (also in this series), is one fine example. Another is Carolus Deane, Senior History Master at Queen's School, Newminster, brought to life (and now, alas, virtually dead) by Leo Bruce, who was Rupert Croft-Cooke, prolific and excellent writer of memoirs. Yet a third was the hero of my own first novel, *Death and the Visiting Firemen*.

But he, though successful enough, I like to think, as a character and as an investigator, did not survive into a next book. With pretty good reason. It is really most unlikely that a school teacher in the course of a professional career no matter of what length would come across more than one body murdered in mysterious circumstances. No, your amateur sleuth has to have either some vague link with the police world, even if it is as slight as being best friends with Major Blank, Chief Constable of Blankshire, or he has to have large private means. Only indeed with the latter will he have the sheer cheek to involve himself in murder case after murder case.

But Hildegarde Withers's incorrigible meddlesomeness (in New York she used to listen to the police radio and hang around Center Street headquarters selling raffle tickets) serves fairly reasonably as a pretext for criminous involvement. If on occasion it does strain credibility, so does her abortive affair with her sparring-partner/colleague, Inspector Oscar Piper. Her cartoon image equally spoils her as any sort of great detective. The Great Detective, though as much a literary artefact, is on a higher plane altogether. He, or she, is not a cartoon figure but a figure of myth.

So Hildegarde Withers is reduced to solving her cases by mere observation. There are clues strewn around which we, the readers, see along with her, and, alas, in this way she must realize their significance only towards the end of a book, even if she does beat us to it by a short head. This is another strike, it must be admitted, against the Withers books.

It is a defect inherent, of course, in all classical detective stories. But it is one that has been overcome in other hands. First, one of the true Great Detectives will in solving a mystery combine factors so unlikely that it is perfectly credible that the case should remain an enigma until the great person has opportunity to enter a trance-like state and emerge with something wholly new. Another classic way of avoiding the dilemma is to endow a detective with a Watson to whom he can with reasonable credibility throw out no more than hints about what he has observed (the dog in the night-time). Or there is the device often used by Agatha Christie, the Koh-i-Noor of the Crime Club, with Hercule Poirot. Poirot will make a series of startling minor discoveries in the course of the story, preserving his status as the omniscient detective, and only at the very end, having thus been pre-proved, is it safe to let him cry of himself, '*Imbécile, imbécile,* thirty-six times *imbécile,*' and rush off to the final unmasking.

However, although I have somewhat disparaged Mr

9

Palmer, it is only fair to say that in his day he had a considerable reputation. He was a favourite author of that king of the American writers of 'English' detective stories, Ellery Queen. He achieved, too, honourable mention as a top exponent of the puzzle story, alongside Erle Stanley Gardner and John Dickson Carr, in a 1937 novel by the dean of American crime critics, Anthony Boucher, *The Case of the Seven of Calvary*. And his fellow authors elected him in 1954 as president of the Mystery Writers of America. He was, as well, a much-employed screen writer, scripting among others the Hollywood Bulldog Drummond films. And, besides all this, he had, one after another, no fewer than five wives as well as maintaining a large collection of model penguins, one of which you will meet in the pages ahead.

CHAPTER 1

'Morning and evening, maids hear the goblins cry . . .'
—CHRISTINA ROSSETTI

Darkness was falling when the girl who called herself Janet Poole came back into her tiny cubicle of an office and pulled the venetian blinds on the dripping California afternoon. From somewhere off across the valley came the rumble of thunder; she shivered, remembering the classic Greek belief that thunder on the left presaged great and terrible events. Or perhaps, she thought, a rabbit must have just run over her future grave.

No, not a rabbit. It would have to have been a bird, a very special Bird. She sighed. It had been a long session downstairs in what they all called the sweat-box; for four hours Jan and a dozen other kindred spirits had been watching a screen on which thousands of pencil sketches moved and jumped and blended. They had been watching the rough animation of what was to be some day *Peter Penguin's Barn Dance*.

They had watched in deadly seriousness the pictured antics of a mad, anti-social penguin in everlasting conflict with an obese but sportive hippopotamus, a malignant hawk wearing a six-shooter and a ten-gallon hat, a fantastic cat with Adolphe Menjou moustaches—all of them born of the ink-bottle, anthropomorphic inhabitants of this Never-Never Land.

One day, with some luck and the expenditure of much sweat and tears, all this would take shape and colour and come alive, come wondrously alive, to sparkle for a few minutes on the nation's movie screens. To that end more than two hundred artists and directors and writers, animators and in-betweeners and cameramen and musicians and cutters, laboured endlessly.

11

'Don't ever ask me *why*!' Jan whispered to herself. But she actually loved being a part of it all, and when she left this pixie world for ever some time next summer—oh, *frabjous* day!—it would be with tears in her eyes and a lump in her throat.

She switched on the lights and then plunged her longish, pleasantly-shaped body down before the drawing-board, which was really a tilted desk-top with a revolving glass plate in the centre now illuminated from beneath. She took a pocket mirror from the top drawer and looked most carefully at herself—the self she had somehow created out of nothing more than good bones and a pair of eyes. This life was hard on the eyes, especially on big blue-violet, slightly myopic eyes. But Jan had made her mind up that she wasn't going to break down and wear glasses until she was thirty—still a reassuring distance away. All the same, it might be a good idea to find out about those contact lens things that did the work and didn't show . . .

The watch on her slim brown wrist said that it was almost six, six o'clock in the evening of a long day which seemed ever longer because of last night. They had stayed much too long parked up there in her car on the top of Lookout Mountain in the white incredible moonlight of Southern California, watching the fabulous jewelled lights of Hollywood and Beverly Hills splashed out beneath them and arguing as only people who know and love one another very dearly can argue. That wonderful, stubborn man! Jan smiled, a warm little-girlish smile that transformed her strong-boned Polska face into momentary loveliness, and then she leaned back and pushed at her mop of ash-blonde hair in a gesture that was all sensuous.

'"Haply I think on thee . . .!"' she whispered, making the words sound new and exciting. The Shakespeare sonnets were all new and exciting to Jan; she had learned about them only recently. Thanks to Guy for opening that door for her, and so many, many other doors too . . .

But there were certain things she would have to prove to him too; things that he could and must learn even from a

12

Polska peasant girl if they were ever to make a good marriage out of it. Jan had few if any delusions, and as her grandmother had said, 'There is more to marriage than four legs in a bed.'

That wonderful, unpredictable man!

Then it was that Jan heard a familiar step coming along the hall, and quickly resumed her usual businesslike expression. She looked up with assumed surprise, to see a roundish masculine face, topped by a ridiculous red beret, peering in her doorway. 'Time to knock off, my sweeting,' it said. 'You are maybe joining us over at the Grotto for a couple of quick ones and maybe a small steak, which I will gladly buy?'

Janet smiled, with carefully rationed warmth. 'Not tonight, Tip. I'm bushed.'

Tip Brown had been top artist and story-man at the cartoon studio for a decade; he was one of the best in a fiercely competitive business, but from where she sat he was as nourishing and dull and wholesome as a dish of oatmeal. Long ago Jan had decided that she liked him the way you like an oversized mongrel puppy who keeps trying to crawl into your lap and lick your face. 'No, really,' she said gently.

'Do you good to laugh and play a little?' Then, as she shook her head, he came closer. 'Okay, can I walk you out to the gate? Want to talk to you about things and stuff.'

'No, Tip. Tonight it's just no dice.'

'Oh? I wonder why. As a matter of fact, I know why. Hark!' Tip put his hand to his ear and pantomimed The Listener . . . and then from across the stretches of the studio street Jan could actually hear the faint tinkle of the piano in the music stage, with an individual touch that she knew full well. It made her heart leap up, and it must have showed in her eyes, for Tip Brown subsided a little and said wearily, 'So that piano-player of yours is on the lot, scoring again, is he? And *you've* got to wait around and drive him home?'

'I don't gotta, I wanna,' Jan flushed. 'And Tip dear, please don't be like that. You'd love Guy if you'd only take the time to know him. Just because he doesn't drive a car

13

is no sign he's not a man, and a lot of man. This part-time music work is terribly important to him, it's already resulted in his getting two songs published in New York based on things he's done here. If you'd only get to know him—'

Tip Brown shook his head. 'My quota of charming young gentlemen is filled,' he said firmly. 'Well, baby, maybe some day you'll learn about musicians the hard way. They eat their young, if any. But everybody to their own taste.'

'Exactly!' said Jan.

Tip Brown looked at her wistfully, then bowed low, vented a shrill Peter Penguin laugh, and then went up the hall a little slower than he had come. Janet sighed—because Tip was really a dear, fun to be with and fun to go out with and if things had been different . . . But things weren't different; things were as they were, and wonderful! And it was only in some of the more outlying parts of Tibet where a woman was permitted more than one husband.

It was six o'clock now, and as if that had been a cue the sound of the distant piano cut off short. Jan felt the day's weariness fall from her like a dropped cloak, and hastily reached into the second drawer of her desk for a handbag, feeling that a little lipstick never hurt a girl at the close of a hard day.

Then it happened. Her searching fingers found something else laid on top of the handbag, something that shouldn't have been there at all. It was only a brown paper envelope with her name imprinted in big red capitals, and below the name a sketch of what everybody in the studio called 'The Bird'—the fantastic penguin who played the starring rôle in most of the films. But this drawing was wrong, all wrong. It showed the beloved, irrepressible Bird with his toes turned up in death, a strangling noose about his throat. Long ago Jan had learned the unwritten laws of cartoondom; no snakes, no cows with udders, no blood and no death—no death, *ever*. The very blackest of its villains, The Big Bad Wolf and Honest John and Buzz Buzzard and all the rest got their come-uppance in the last reel, but even they always lived on to plot again some other day. This was a world of

14

laughter, and laughter and death don't mix.

The picture was just one of the things you *didn't* draw, not even while doodling in fun. Jan was about to throw the envelope away when she found that inside there was a sheet of drawing paper cut into the shape of a heart; it was a valentine, the message printed with hot red crayon:

'TO THE NUDE ARTISTS' MODEL:
COME AND TRIP IT AS YOU GO,
YOU ARE GOING TO DIE, YOU KNOW,
WILLY-NILLY FALL IN LINE
AND BE IN DEATH MY VALENTINE!
LUCY.'

Jan's 'O-o-oh' of surprise was thin and reedy, but it must have carried down the hall, for a moment later Tip Brown in his raincoat came plunging in the doorway and saw her viciously tearing bits of paper into smaller bits and hurling them into the wastebasket.

'*Nothing's* the matter!' she cried at him. 'Please go away!' But Tip stood there, bug-eyed and motionless. Suddenly she stood up, overturning her chair, and went out and down the hall with coat and hat clutched in one hand and bag in the other, hurrying faster and faster towards the stair. Soon she was running headlong, down the steps and out into the lighted, rainswept studio street, and then breathlessly on and on towards the doorway of the music stage and the safety of Guy's waiting arms.

CHAPTER 2

'Do not men die fast enough without being destroyed by each other?'

— TELEMACHUS

'There seem to have been at least three of these nasty things delivered to people in our studio yesterday,' the unexpected visitor was saying. 'Or rather, left for them to find. One

15

turned up this morning on the desk of our musical director, a volatile Slovak, who blew his top and was no good for the rest of the day. Naturally we don't like it.' The man didn't look as if he liked anything very much; he wore a thin face, thinner hair, and a tight mouth. He had originally introduced himself as Ralph Cushak, studio production manager, and it was fairly clear from his manner that, at least at the moment, he was acting under orders with which he did not entirely agree.

Across the little Hollywood bungalow sitting-room his hostess, an angular spinster of uncertain years but certain temperament, was feeling flattered but a little confused. She had had her crowded hours back in Manhattan; now she chafed at this enforced retirement to the bland monotonous climate of Southern California though her asthma made it indicated. But like an ageing fire-horse her ears pricked up at the sound of the siren. 'Perhaps if I could see one of these un-comic valentines?' she suggested. Then, as he hesitated, she continued, 'Heavens to Betsy, young man! Don't you worry about my sensibilities. Anyone who has been a teacher in the public schools of New York as long as I have is not easily shocked; I have washed many little mouths out with soap, and erased all sorts of words from the blackboard.'

'I see,' said Mr Cushak cautiously. 'Well, as to the warnings or threats or whatever they were, the recipients claim to have destroyed them. However, from what I can learn, the messages seem not to have been actually obscene. But I gather that there was something of a most unpleasant nature in each one, some personal stab below the belt.'

'But why come to me?' Miss Hildegarde Withers asked, not unreasonably. 'You have said that the paper and envelopes were studio stationery. It is most obviously an inside job, and I know little or nothing about movie studios. You see, I'm only an amateur snoop at best; I have no licence or anything.'

'Yet you seem to have been highly recommended by the police.'

Miss Withers's long lantern-face was quizzical. 'And since

when have the Los Angeles police, with whom I had a slight disagreement some years ago,* gone around recommending retired schoolteachers for this sort of delicate assignment?' She sniffed audibly.

'They didn't,' Cushak admitted. 'Our studio is located outside of the legal limits of Los Angeles anyway, and the local force is no worse and no better than one would expect. If we called them in they'd rampage through the place, browbeat a lot of our people, and get absolutely nowhere. The story would also leak out to the newspapers. In the motion picture industry we try to wash our own dirty linen without any fanfare of trumpets, and if sometimes we do happen to have a rotten apple in the barrel we feel it should be quietly nipped in the bud without spotlights or the setting off of Roman candles . . .' He ran out of words and out of breath, hopelessly lost amid his own metaphors.

'Well, then?'

'The mention of your name came from New York,' he admitted. 'You see, our cartoon studio is really a separate entity inside Miracle-Paradox. They release our pictures, but our shop is independently owned and managed, with our own buildings on a corner of the big lot. Our big boss—' here Cushak paused and seemed about to genuflect three times towards the east—'our big boss is back in New York on a business trip. He was advised of this situation over long distance, and he told me to contact you; it seems he had heard of you through some big-shot police official he met at a luncheon.'

'*Dear* Inspector Oscar Piper,' said the schoolteacher, brightening visibly. 'He's always trying to throw a job my way, as long as it keeps me out of *his* way. But please do go on.'

Mr Cushak came straight to the point. 'This sort of problem is supposed to be right up your alley. Of course, at the studio we have our own security force—mostly retired cops—but they're trained to handle pilferers and gate-

The Puzzle of the Blue Banderilla

crashers; nothing like this. You'll have to be there on the lot to be able to function. Would it be convenient for you to report to the main gate at nine o'clock tomorrow morning? There'll be a pass waiting.'

'Not quite so fast,' objected Miss Withers sensibly. 'While I admit that I like to meddle in problems of a criminal nature as a sort of mental exercise, I have in the past worked almost entirely on murder cases. I'm not at all sure—'

'We need you,' Cushak told her, obviously remembering his orders. 'And there was really a very definite death threat in each of the poison-pen valentines. Perhaps there is no actual danger to anybody, but we want to find out who is responsible for this, and *quick*.'

The schoolteacher was still dubious. 'From my experience and from what I have read on the subject, I'd say that murderers rarely rattle before they strike. A person intending to commit homicide doesn't draw silly pictures and write warning messages to put his victims on guard. This looks to me like a bad practical joke.' She cocked her head. 'Do you have any practical jokers at your studio?'

Cushak's tight mouth tightened tighter. 'We are lousy with them, ma'am—if you'll pardon the expression. It's practically an occupational disease among our artists, gagmen, directors and writers; their minds are frivolous and run in that channel for some reason. Irresponsible children, all of them.' It was fairly clear that Mr Cushak sincerely wished that movie cartoons could somehow be put together by bright young certified public accountants who punched the time-clock on the dot and always cleaned up their desks before going home at night. 'They are always raising some sort of hell,' he told her. 'Like putting gin in the water-coolers. You might not believe it, but one day last winter after I had had to announce that there would be no Christmas bonus because of retrenchment, I came down to my brand-new Cadillac on the studio parking lot and found a wheelbarrow brimming full of water in the back seat! What, may I ask, can one do with a wheelbarrow full of water? It took me over an hour to dip it out with a tin can,

18

and I was late for an appointment with my analyst.'

With some effort Miss Withers restrained a smile, but this was no time to indoctrinate the man about the principle of the siphon. 'And have you any idea as to the identity of the culprit?'

'I have. I can't prove anything, but it's just the sort of thing that Larry Reed would think of. He's a very brilliant artist or he wouldn't stay on the payroll, but he's erratic and temperamental and always pulling fast ones.'

'Such as?'

'Well, one year we had an efficiency expert on the lot, not very popular with our personnel as you can imagine. Reed took it upon himself to insert a newspaper ad. on the 26th of December, giving this poor chap's home address and offering a dollar apiece for used Christmas trees. All over greater Los Angeles gullible people saw the ad. and pulled off the decorations and the tinsel and hauled their trees out to his house, and when they found it was a false alarm some of them became rather violent. They also dumped the unwanted trees in his front yard; I believe he wound up with several hundred of them.'

'How gay and delightful,' murmured Miss Withers. 'But not very.'

'And Larry Reed pulled another gag,' Cushak went on in an aggrieved tone. 'He'd had a slight run-in with Tip Brown, one of the other top artists at the studio, and got even with him by filling out a phoney change-of-address slip at the post office. Brown didn't get any mail at all for weeks. He missed his bills, and had his utilities cut off for non-payment. He also I believe missed certain important letters of a romantic nature. Finally he checked, and found that everything had been forwarded to Horsecollar, Arizona, to be held until called for. Of course Brown got all his mail eventually, but he was somewhat bitter about it at the time.'

'I see,' said the schoolteacher thoughtfully. 'Practical jokes—and they're usually most impractical, too. Like pulling a chair out from somebody about to sit down, and perhaps fracturing a pelvis.'

He nodded. 'The artistic temperament, blowing off steam. Sometimes I feel like the keeper in a snake-pit. But I still don't see how Reed could have had anything to do with our present problem, because as it happened he checked out of the studio early yesterday morning, pleading illness. Probably just another of his hangovers, but he certainly wasn't around where he could have planted those nasty valentines.'

Miss Withers said nothing, but she looked very thoughtful. 'Anyway,' the studio executive said firmly, 'the big boss wants very much to find out who is responsible for this latest and most unfunniest gag—if it is a gag. And it's clearly an inside job; it must be attacked from inside. My instructions are to hire you, to add you to our staff on some plausible pretext or other, and get you inside the gates where you can have a free rein.'

'You actually mean that you want me to pass as a regular studio employee?' She brightened. 'I used to paint china in my girlhood days; perhaps I could make like one of your artists?'

Mr Cushak looked politely dubious. 'There is,' he said, 'a considerable difference between china-painting and drawing cartoons. Do you happen to play any musical instrument? We often hire outside musicians. And sometimes we hire actors too—but no, I don't think your voice would do even for Wilma Wombat. We'll have to hit on something else—' He broke off, looking towards the patio door. 'What on *earth*,' he gasped, 'is *that* thing?'

Something large and brownish, rather resembling a bear who had got caught in a buzz-saw, was standing outside on its hind legs and trying to twist the door-knob with its teeth. After a moment the creature succeeded and came scampering in, a great, galumphing beast; on closer view it was a dog, but a dog fearfully and wonderfully made. It was about to hurl itself upon the visitor when Miss Withers spoke sharply. 'Talley, mind your manners! This is Mr Cushak—Mr Cushak, this is Talleyrand, my Standard French poodle.'

The dog, a sworn friend of the entire human race, restrained himself with difficulty from climbing into the visitor's lap and licking his face; he compromised by sitting down and offering a hopeful paw. Cushak shook it, murmuring an automatic 'How do you do?' and then his face slowly lighted up with inspiration.

'I *have* it!' he said.

'You have what?' queried the schoolteacher blankly.

'An idea! This makes everything easy. A poodle—we'll hire *him* and you can come along as chaperone.' Cushak went on to explain that for some years the studio had been fooling around with the idea of a feature-length cartoon which would have a poodle as its hero; the project had been shelved but it could be ostensibly taken out of moth-balls and put back into production, with Talley as the model for the artists to work from.

'A *live* model?' gasped Miss Withers. 'For cartoons?'

Mr Cushak explained that it was common practice in the business; that in the past they had had kangaroos and raccoons and even a baby alligator on the lot for the artists to sketch. 'Nobody in the studio,' he said firmly, 'will think anything of it. The dog is a natural comedian anyway. You'll both be there at nine?'

'Wild horses,' decided the schoolteacher, 'couldn't keep us away.'

'Good, good.' So it was settled with a handshake.

It wasn't, Miss Withers admitted to herself after the man had taken himself away in his shining Cadillac, exactly the sort of case she would have chosen. But at least it was one where her services had been requested and would presumably be paid for—a very pleasant novelty in her career as a sleuth. And she felt that she was coming up with one of her famous hunches. 'It would be rather a feather in our caps, wouldn't it,' she asked the adoring poodle a little later, 'if we could walk into Mr Cushak's office at the studio bright and early tomorrow morning with this case all neatly tied up in a bag? We shall set the alarm for seven.'

At nine o'clock next morning Miss Hildegarde Withers

21

appeared at the main entrance of Miracle-Paradox Studios complete with leashed poodle and also an unleashed headache, a headache beyond all aspirin. She went through the necessary formalities at the gate; getting inside the studio was about as difficult as getting into Fort Knox—and then the private policeman behind the wicket found her pass and she was guided by a cute blue-uniformed messenger girl past looming sound-stages, past bungalows and office buildings and standing sets all beautiful in front and plaster and chicken-wire behind, until finally they came to the back corner lot and the street called Cartoon Alley. She was led up to Mr Cushak's office in a smallish modernistic two-storey building and plunked down in a reception-room decorated with brightly-coloured pictures of animals wearing pants—prominent among them was the engaging Bird known as Peter Penguin . . .

The schoolteacher cooled her heels and whiled away the time by watching Mr Cushak's secretary, a lush, slightly-overblown girl with midnight hair and a most plunging neckline, who juggled the phone and the inter-office communicator most deftly and at the same time managed to open the morning mail and write half a dozen letters. Now and then she went out to the coffee-vending machine in the hall, as if she needed it. There were dark shadows around her eyes.

'Burning the candle at both ends and in the middle too,' thought the schoolteacher.

And then a buzzer sounded and she was told that she might go on into the Presence. It was something like an audience with the Pope, she gathered, except that of course you didn't actually have to wear a veil and a black dress. She tiptoed gingerly inside, and found Mr Cushak smiling his usual thin smile. 'Fine, fine,' he said. 'You're here.'

There was no denying that, so she didn't try. But she took a deep breath. 'Mr Cushak, there's something—'

'Oh, yes,' he interrupted. 'The remuneration. Shall we say $250 a week for the poodle and $100 for you as caretaker, with a bonus of course if successful? We'll make it a three week guarantee; you should be able to wind it up in that time, no?'

'But—' Miss Withers began protestingly.

He waved his hand. 'Okay, make it $200 for you, and that's as far as we can go. Motion picture studios have their problems today, dear lady, what with switching to three-dimension and with television breathing on our necks.' He spoke the word 'television' as if it had four letters and was something written by nasty children on walls and sidewalks.

'Thank you, the stipend is most adequate,' she said hastily. 'I was not holding out for more money; the novelty of being paid anything at all for my humble services is enough. But you see, Mr Cushak, I thought last night that I might wind up your little mystery in one day. "Pride goeth —" It seemed obvious to me that the person we sought was somebody on your staff, one of your wild Bohemian artist-writers who had slipped a cog. In other words, a habitual practical joker who had gone too far and ventured across the line of good sense and good taste. You yourself mentioned one name.'

'Larry Reed?' Mr Cushak looked blank. 'But I told you that Reed was home sick that day, and yesterday too. It would have been impossible for him to have planted those nasty valentines. Which reminds me.' He pressed a button on his talk-box. 'Joyce? Get me the cashier's office.' There was a moment's pause, and then—'Cushak here. Larry Reed hasn't reported for work again today, or phoned in. No hangover should last three days, so I want him terminated and a final cheque made out as of today. That's right.' He hung up, and turned back to his visitor with a look in his eye which indicated that he was remembering a certain wheelbarrow full of water in a certain automobile. 'We have to be firm with these people sometimes,' he explained. 'And Larry Reed has finally gone too far.'

'Further than you think,' murmured Miss Withers. 'You see—well, I'll have to begin at the beginning and go on to the end and then stop, as it says in *Alice*. As usual, I have

23

been leaping to conclusions. Last night I had it all figured out that Larry Reed could have found ways to strew the poison-pen valentines around without actually being present in the studio, that his absence could have been contrived. A girlfriend, an accomplice perhaps.'

Cushak thought, and shook his head. 'I doubt it. Though from what I understand he has girlfriends enough around the place and even an ex-wife—Joyce Reed—who happens to be my secretary and a good one too. They divorced a couple of years ago, but they seem to have stayed on reasonably friendly terms. But not that friendly—if Reed did think of anything so demented as sending out vicious valentines to people in the studio he wouldn't have taken her or anybody else in on the deal. And for all his twisted sense of humour, I don't think that he or any of our people would possibly have thought of drawing Peter Penguin *dead*. His mind just wouldn't work that way.'

She nodded. 'I live and learn. But at the time Reed did seem like the most promising suspect. So bright and early this morning I looked up his home address in the phone book and then took pains to pay him a call, a surprise visit, working on the old but sound theory that people wakened from a sound sleep are usually very poor liars when confronted with a sudden accusation. I thought that I might by that means solve our little mystery ahead of time, but—' She sniffed.

'Well, I see that the ruse didn't succeed.' Cushak shrugged his well-padded shoulders. 'Anyway, you have eliminated Reed, which is that much gained.'

'Correction please,' said the maiden schoolteacher gently. 'I didn't eliminate Larry Reed, but I'm afraid that someone else did. Because I found him very dead.'

CHAPTER 3

'Life so strange, so sad the sky . . .'
— SWINBURNE

It had been like this. Shortly after dawn Miss Withers
had located Larry Reed's home on the eastern fringes of
Mulholland Drive, that winding pathway atop the low
brush-covered mountains that divide Beverly Hills and
Hollywood from the Valley, and had turned her sputtering
little coupé into a long driveway leading down to a coral-pink
house perched precariously on the edge of a canyon; it was
a lonely house without a neighbour in view, its modern
crackerbox lines stark and bare in the bright white light of
the morning.

A big Buick convertible of recent date had been parked
hastily or carelessly with one wheel in the petunia beds, its
keys still dangling from the dashboard. Yet the mud on the
tyres was dry. Outside the front door were newspapers
and bottles of milk and yoghurt. Nobody answered Miss
Withers's ring at the bell, but when she put her sharp ear
to the panel she could hear far away inside a muffled
intermittent yowling, as of some trapped animal in pain.

'A cat is in trouble,' decided the schoolteacher. The dog
Talley was elaborately disinterested, perhaps because sad
experience had taught him that anything happening to
cats was much too good for them. Leaving the poodle to
investigate some interesting bushes, she made her way
around to the other side of the house, which was really the
front. The place gave on to a wide brick patio on the very
brim of the canyon, cluttered with barbecue equipment and
ping-pong tables and summer furniture all covered with
leaves and dust. There was a most breath-taking view of
the whole San Fernando Valley and of the Santa Rosa
mountains to the north; it was a place someone had loved

25

and then neglected; the roses should have been cut back and the grass of the tiny lawn sadly needed mowing.

Through picture windows Miss Withers could glimpse a big living-room, cold and empty now. The french doors were locked, but locks could sometimes yield to a deft bit of work with a bent hairpin. It was of course technically breaking-and-entering, but to the schoolteacher the piteous appeals of an animal in distress could excuse a great deal. The distant yowling still went on, a tired mechanical sound now. She hesitated only for a second.

The lock gave easily, and she went inside. 'Is anybody home?' she cried, and when there was no answer she advanced into the living-room. It was completely a man's room, smelling of stale tobacco, furnished expensively and haphazardly with more than the usual complement of lamps and lounge chairs and ashtrays. The books on the shelves were mostly texts on art or bound art-studies, etchings and reproductions of Picasso and Klee and Degas and Dali, an oddly assorted lot which told the curious schoolteacher nothing in particular. In one corner was an easel holding an unfinished watercolour, the bust portrait of a girl with interesting cheek-bones and unusual eyes; she thought it rather remarkably good. Nearby were other stacked pictures finished and half-finished; drawings, oils, pastels, all splashy and improvised and short on technique according to her conservative tenets, but showing that Larry Reed had moments when he wanted most desperately to be something more than a comic cartoonist.

The place was silent now, but she kept on exploring. On the left was a kitchen, full of labour-saving gadgets but a bit dusty. There were the remains of a breakfast on the dinette table, relics of ham and eggs, potatoes and toast and orange juice and coffee—not, she judged, today's vintage nor yesterday's. It was typically a bachelor's kitchen, the contents of shelves and refrigerator leaning largely towards beer and fizz-water and the makings of breakfast and late midnight snacks; it had only known the casual ministrations of a part-time cleaning woman who hadn't been in recently.

26

'Men who live alone!' sniffed Miss Withers. She doggedly continued her explorations, still seeking the source of that muffled howling. Turning from the kitchen, she came into a little hallway opening into a sybaritic bathroom with a black sunken tub, with big fuzzy towels marked 'His', 'Theirs' and 'Its', and a wall-cabinet overflowing with medicines, ointments, mouth-washes and vitamin pills—a veritable pharmacopœia. The roll of toilet tissue was imprinted with gay jokes, purple limericks and La Parisienne drawings; when it was touched a concealed music-box played 'Sweet Violets', which caused the schoolteacher to sniff a disapproving sniff.

There remained only the bedroom, which she entered with mounting apprehension. It was a big room, dim even in this early morning sunshine since the blinds were all drawn tight. The bedside phone suddenly started to yowl again; belatedly Miss Withers recognized it as the signal the telephone exchange sends out over the line when a receiver is left off the hook. No cats in trouble, anyway, she said to herself with relief. And then she saw it.

On an oversized, rumpled bed a man was lying, twisted and contorted. He was fully dressed in expensive, carefully-chosen sports clothes; he had evidently ended the hard way. He was a big man in his thirties with curly, rumpled hair; he had died strangling, groping blindly for the telephone. 'Swelled up like a poisoned pup,' whispered the schoolteacher, backing sensibly and hastily out of the room and hoping that she had left no fingerprints anywhere. She tiptoed out of the lonely house of death and made her way hastily back to her car, collecting Talley on the way.

'Here we go again,' she said to the dog. 'Hold on to your hat.'

At any rate, as she told Mr Cushak in his office a little later, it was no false alarm.

The studio executive swallowed, looking rather pale around the gills. 'But—I can hardly believe it! This is impossible. No signs of violence, you say? Then it must just

27

be an unfortunate coincidence; Reed had a heart attack and died a natural death.'

'The death,' Miss Withers advised him coldly, 'was most unnatural from where I sit. I have no pretensions to being a pathologist, but the evidence is fairly clear. Reed was in excellent health and appetite and ate a copious breakfast day before yesterday. He came in to work, was taken suddenly ill, and rushed home to die there alone.'

'But—but how can this tie in? I mean, Reed didn't even *receive* one of the valentines!'

Miss Withers shrugged her shoulders, then pulled Talley the poodle out of Mr Cushak's wastebasket where the dog had been hopefully foraging. 'There is more to this than meets the eye,' she said. 'But I would very much like a chance to snoop around Larry Reed's office or studio or whatever you call it before the police get here.'

Cushak winced. 'Why—his office was number 12 in the building across the street, on the second floor. His name is on the door. But—'

'And I want a chance to meet all the people who got the poison-pen valentines.'

'Very well. Of course. But—but you just mentioned the police. I suppose—yes, I must call them and report this.'

She gave him a mildly withering look. 'I've already taken care of that; I stopped and phoned them on my way here, somewhat anonymously. Naturally I didn't care at this particular time to be locked up as a material witness and I had no real right to be in the house anyway, so I'm afraid I intimated that I was the cleaning-woman. Anyway, they have been alerted, and will do what has to be done. Now, if you don't mind, I think I'll have a look at that office.'

Cushak nodded slowly. 'Very well. You might even take over the office as a base of operations. I'll arrange it. And I'll assign one of our best writer-artists to work with you on the poodle story. If there's anything else you need—'

There was a great deal else, but the schoolteacher wasn't sure just what. She left Mr Cushak staring moodily at his desk blotter and then led Talleyrand out of the office. They crossed Cartoon Alley, the wide street already bustling with a most bewildering complexity of activities, and entered the box-like office building across the way. It took Miss Withers some time to locate the cubicle that had been Larry Reed's, for his name had already been erased from the door. An elderly gnome in coveralls was turning out the place at the moment. Pictures, books, pipes and tobacco—art materials, an amazingly complete collection of handy home remedies such as cough syrup and mineral oil and bicarbonate and milk of magnesia and vitamin pills—everything was all being tumbled into paper cartons, helter-skelter.

'So *soon?*' gasped Miss Withers from the doorway.

The old man looked up in ghoulish glee. 'Well, he got fired, didn't he?' He nodded wisely. 'They all get it sooner or later, and from where I sit the sooner the better. Playboy parasites, all of them.'

'You sound bitter, Mr—?'

'Cassidy it is. Pop Cassidy, they call me now when they send me on errands. Once it was Jonathan H. Cassidy and I had my own bungalow on this lot. I been with the studio since it started with Uncle Carl working on a shoestring and making better pictures than anybody knows how to do nowadays, with all their wide-screens and three-dimensions and stuff. But they ruined movies when sound came in.' He came closer, a gap-toothed grin on his face. 'Lady, I was a director in those days, believe it or not. Sound came in and they threw away action and pantomime for talk, talk, talk —they went and hired directors from Broadway plays and I went out with a knife between my shoulder-blades. But everybody in this business gets that sooner or later.' He deftly slid the two filled cartons out into the hall. 'You the new one coming in?'

Miss Withers started. 'Why—why yes, in a way I suppose I am.'

'It's a sorta madhouse,' confided the old man. 'But maybe you'll get used to it if you last long enough. Most don't.' He went out, leaving Miss Withers and the poodle alone in the bare little office. She sat down at the big tilted desk, switched the light off and on, and almost reached for the phone. Then she hesitated. Would her somewhat anomalous position here at the studio justify the expense of a long-distance call to New York?

Yet it was a time when she would have much appreciated the advice of her old friend and sparring-partner, the Inspector. She thought about it from all angles, but it was hard to concentrate here in this little room, its walls crowded with great oblong sheets of framed cardboard on which there had been pinned hundreds of rough pencil sketches of something called *Peter Penguin Nightmare*, a thing full of sharks and crocodiles. This cartoon world seemed to have a different set of laws and traditions and a language all its own; to the schoolteacher it was an uncharted sea with rocks just beneath the surface, inhabited by anthropomorphic monsters leering crazily at her. Yet as she studied the drawings it all seemed to be beginning to make a sort of twisted sense.

One of the cartoon characters swallowed a pistol, and every time he hiccoughed a shot was fired, never of course hitting anybody. A hippopotamus in green pants walked the plank of a pirate schooner; walked straight out into thin air and then back again to shout, 'Avast, ye squabs!' at his bewildered persecutors. A scared rabbit, startled from its little ramble-shack in the hills, turned its ears into propeller-blades and took off gaily into the wild blue yonder.

Never-Never Land. How on earth could a retired schoolteacher cope with people who thought in these formalized, wildly-exaggerated terms? If they were capable of this they'd be capable of anything . . . It was a real relief to her some time later when her solitude was broken by the advent of a large, wholesome-looking man who introduced himself as Tip Brown. He was a bulky, solid, pink-faced man in his late thirties with a militantly boyish haircut and blunt, clever hands; he explained a bit diffidently that for his sins he had been sentenced to drop everything else and work here with her. Miss Withers liked him on sight—and for that reason mistrusted him too, not being overly sure of first impressions.

After him came two studio workmen carrying a story-board still grimy from the dust of the cellar vaults, and titled *The Circus Poodle*. It was hung on the wall facing her desk, replacing one of the others.

Tip Brown looked at her quizzically. 'You an old hand at this business?'

'A very new hand, a neophyte,' Miss Withers confessed.

'Then I guess I'd better explain,' he said. He did explain with painstaking weariness, that each of the drawings pinned to the story-board in this preliminary stage was supposed to represent a master-scene in the picture, a high spot in the story. Other artists would later fill in the blanks between, which was why they were called 'in-betweens'. There were also the animators, who made the drawings that the original creators hadn't bothered with—making things move and come alive.

'It's a sort of complicated business, in case you didn't know,' Tip Brown confided. 'We do it over and over again, and never know just where we're coming out.' He slumped in an easy-chair by the window, a cold pipe dangling from his mouth, eyeing Miss Withers and Talley too with a certain amount of puzzled wonder. But he was game, and shook Talley's paw as often as it was offered. 'So we're going to have another whirl at the Circus Poodle headache,' he said. 'It's a mystery to me why the front office wants to dig up this one; it was a good story idea but somewhere it curdled. Anyhow, here we go, you and I and the pup. Do you *have* to sit in my lap, dog?' He gently shoved Talley to the floor. 'And we're in Larry Reed's old office, too. He got the quick axe, I hear.'

'So I understood,' said the schoolteacher cautiously.

'And now *you* get your name on the door, eh? You must know where the body is buried.'

'But it isn't even—' The schoolteacher bit her lip, realizing that the man was only speaking in the vernacular, trying to put a newcomer at her ease. He had already taken out sketch-pad and pencil, and was studying Talleyrand.

'You supposed to work with me on the new story-line, or

31

are you just here with the pup?' Tip wanted to know. Miss Withers cautiously admitted that she was not quite sure what her duties at the studio would amount to. The artist wryly said that sometimes nobody was sure. He prodded the poodle gently with an expensive oxford. 'Can the beast do any tricks?'

Talleyrand, who like all his breed had been born to the grease-paint and cap-and-bells of the clown, was delighted to show off his not inconsiderable repertoire. Tip Brown, somewhat visibly impressed, dashed off half a hundred sketches, pure simplified line and mass, that got the big dog down on paper as no camera could ever have done; it was, Miss Withers realized as she peeked over the artist's shoulder, the veritable essence of poodle. Evidently the young man liked to talk while he worked. 'You see, ma'am, the story of *The Circus Poodle* is this; we start with this pampered pooch who belongs to a rich woman, elderly and eccentric, a sort of Hetty Green type . . .'

The schoolteacher suddenly realized that he was now sketching her, and not the dog at all. She bristled a little, but Tip Brown went blithely on: 'This old biddy with her millions, she's practically on her death-bed and because she may pop off any minute her ever-loving nieces and nephews being to cluster around like vultures, none of them worth a hoot in hell but all hot-pants after a legacy. She can't stand 'em, so on a whim she makes a will leaving everything in trust to the dog, who sleeps on a featherbed and eats only caviare and porterhouse steaks.'

'Yes, I see. But—'

'In this first sequence the poodle is clipped in the old-fashioned phony way, with pompoms on its legs and a ribbon in its hair—pampered darling stuff.' Tip's pencil was flying, illustrating his words. A pile of discarded sheets began to pile up untidily on the floor beside him. 'The heirs —I mean the ones who thought they'd inherit—don't care much for losing out to a lap-dog, so they have a conference and decide to slip Cuddles or whatever his name is some Rough-on-Rats in his afternoon tea. Only they forget the family parrot is in the room where they foment the dire plot. He is a character, a busybody, and he waits his chance and gleefully tips off the whole thing to the dog. So the poodle does a double-take and saves his precious skin by turning down the tea and jumping head-first out of the window. He goes off on the town, where he has a rough time of it too.'

'Porterhouse steaks are difficult to come by, these days,' admitted Miss Withers.

'Check, sister. Even at my salary I eat at hamburger joints, mostly.'

'You're not married, Mr Brown?'

He looked up from his pad. 'No, ma'am, not currently.'

'What a shame to have a nice eligible bachelor going to waste, so to speak. Of course I speak only as a confirmed spinster who abhors that sort of thing. No prospects?'

'Huh? Why—' Tip Brown hesitated.

'There are lots of pretty girls around the studio. The secretary in Mr Cushak's office seemed to me to be the type who'd be attractive to men . . .'

'Joyce?' He laughed. 'The man-eater? Oh, I admit that once I gave her a slight whirl. But it's my private opinion that underneath it all she's still carrying a torch for Larry Reed; she was married to him for a while some time back. Anyway, we had a lot of laughs but we didn't hit it off. But I'll admit—' Here Tip Brown grinned almost sheepishly —'I'll admit that there is a long tall blonde on this lot with whom I would willingly make a trip to the altar on ten minutes' notice. But she seems to prefer musicians, dammit.' He sighed.

'"Faint heart . . ."' quoted Miss Withers, ever the hopeful matchmaker. 'Why don't you send her flowers?'

'I'd rather send that musician some henbane blossoms,' Tip said fervently. 'Him and his fancy Harvard accent! But enough of my broken heart. To get back to the epic—the poodle lives out of garbage cans and picks up a few pennies by dancing on street corners. His coat grows out so he looks like a sheep-dog. Winter is here and he almost freezes;

comedy-pathos stuff with icicles goes in here. Comes early spring and it's time for Jingling Brothers' Circus to open at Madison Square Garden—or maybe we have it somewhere in the suburbs under the big top. Anyway the pup drifts in and hangs around the mess-tent, half-starved and looking for a handout. Comedy scene where he looks at an elephant and thinks he could eat it at a meal. Finally the ringmaster sees him and figures an angle. I guess the ringmaster would be Willy Wombat—no, Harry Hawk would be better, with a sneer and a blacksnake whip. Sam and Sally Sparrow are aerialists, Herman Hippo is the clown. The poodle is given a new screwy haircut like this one—'

'A Dutch bob,' explained the schoolteacher stiffly. 'The modern trim for the breed, only it's still not accepted by the judges at dog-shows. Not that I'd put my Talley into a dog-show anyway . . .'

'Okay. And they work the poodle into the circus as a clown, acrobat, roustabout, anything. He has a hard life, but some of the other performers befriend him. We introduce a rhinoceros fat lady or better still a chimpanzee who plays in the band and rides a bicycle on the high-wire . . .'

It all began to sound to Miss Withers like an off-key version of *Toby Tyler or Ten Weeks with the Circus*, a juvenile classic of her distant childhood. But before she could say so, the phone burst into life. Tip Brown leaped hopefully to answer it, and then with some disappointment informed her that Mr Cushak's office was on the line and would she please be in his office for a conference at two sharp?

'Tell them I'll be there,' promised the schoolteacher. 'But I'll make no guarantee as to sharpness.' For as yet in this mad affair there had been so little on which to whet the edge of her mind . . .

Talley the poodle was by this time getting restive and sniffing suggestively around the door. Tip Brown obligingly decided that he could use some outdoor action sketches and borrowed the delighted dog for a romp on the studio lawns, so Miss Withers was left alone with her thoughts of which —as the old saying goes—she had a complete set. She must of course feel her way carefully on this unaccustomed thin ice; she must try to find out what made these people tick, and for that reason she had probed a bit at Mr Brown. He had been open enough—almost too open.

She was naturally burning also with a desire to know what was not going on in that coral-pink house up on Mulholland; police and coroners and medical examiners would be performing their grim but necessary rites. She'd have given almost anything for a front seat—because while in her time she had seen more than a few dead bodies, she had never seen anything like Larry Reed's remains and never wanted to again.

Around noontime the cluttered walls of the little office began to close in upon her. She went outside on a tour of exploration, got herself thoroughly lost among the looming sound-stages and outdoor standing sets, and finally located the studio commissary where she had a modest sandwich and a cup of tea in the midst of all the tinsel glamour of stars and starlets in make-up, dress-extras in evening clothes with smudged handkerchiefs around their collars, executives and agents and office-people, most of whom seemed quite normal and pleasant and everydayish at close range.

She noted that Alan Ladd was not quite as tall but certainly quite as handsome as she had previously imagined, that Abbott and Costello lunched quietly without throwing any dishes at each other, and Piper Laurie was a pixie and Esther Williams a sexy Madonna. There were many other faces at the tables whom she recognized vaguely, having been an inveterate movie-goer for years; they were faces out of the past, once famous, once spotlighted, and now still working at the only job they knew. This was the present, and she had a present-day problem, a monkey on her shoulder.

Who had killed Larry Reed, and why?

There were afternoon papers on sale at the cashier's desk when she paid her modest check, but nothing in the headlines as yet about Reed. There would hardly, she realized, have been time. These papers must have gone to

35

press long before her call to the police, notifying them of the body in the lonely house on Mulholland.

When she finally found her way back to her office she found it empty; evidently Tip Brown had taken Talley with him somewhere for lunch. Miss Withers hoped that the dog would remember his manners and not beg for a second raw hamburger; she had been trying vainly for years to get him to understand that grown dogs eat but once a day. Outside in the hall the cartons packed with Larry Reed's belongings still stood; she poked absently through the litter and found nothing that could be in the least considered a clue, though already a bit of looting had begun. She noted the absence of an imported briar pipe, a bottle of mineral oil, and a big box of expensive anti-histamine tablets that she had seen previously. Perhaps the news of Larry's passing had got around and somebody had thought that they needed a souvenir to remember him by; most certainly somebody else had hated him enough to assist him in prematurely shuffling off this mortal coil. For she was increasingly certain that this was murder, and an odd murder.

Sitting alone at the desk, she fell to aimless doodling with pencil and pad, but her drawings insisted on taking on ugly, twisted shapes. Something in the room annoyed her, setting her teeth on edge; she finally realized that the story-board on the opposite wall was tilted. Automatically she rose to set it level again; nothing bothered her more than an askew picture. But as she touched the board something slipped out from behind it to slither to the floor. It was a brown paper envelope with Larry Reed's name in red crayon—and also bearing the drawing of a dead penguin. She gasped. So Larry Reed had had his warning after all, even though he'd never found it!

Without the slightest compunction Miss Withers tore open the envelope, discovering a heart-shaped piece of drawing paper with hastily-scrawled printing as follows:

'TO THE CARD-CHEAT:
YOU ARE GOING TO GET THE BIRD,

36

DEATH WILL HAVE THE FINAL WORD,
FANCY BOY. YOU'LL SOON BE MINE,
MY STONE STONE STONE-COLD VALENTINE
LUCY.'

The schoolteacher put the thing down, and wiped off her fingers with a handkerchief. Murder, as she well knew, was often nasty and distorted, but not this way—not mixed up with valentines and doggerel verse!

It just didn't make sense. Why should a murderer take all this trouble of drawing pictures and writing verses and leaving warnings? She pondered this for a while, and came out by the same door as she had entered in by.

At precisely two p.m. she showed up at Mr Cushak's office. The girl at the desk looked up and smiled. 'Miss Withers?'

'Yes, Joyce. A command performance.'

The girl smiled wider. 'I'm not Joyce; she took off sick a couple of hours ago and I was called from stenographic to take over. I'm Mabel.'

On second look Miss Withers realized that this one was a little less lush, and with a somewhat different hair-do—though they could both have been poured out of the same mould. 'Well, Mabel—is he in?'

Mabel buzzed and spoke briefly into the talk-box. A moment later Mr Cushak popped out of his office.

He looked for once almost pleased with himself. 'I've got them all waiting inside,' he said. 'I mean, all the people who received those blasted valentines.'

'Oh, *no*!' she exploded.

'Why not?' His face went blank. 'After all, it's only for their own protection. And you said you wanted to meet them.'

She gave him a withering look and then explained wearily, 'Mr Cushak, I wanted to meet them individually, by seeming happenstance, under innocent auspices. I had hoped that in that manner I might just possibly ferret out some useful information. You have inadvertently tipped our hand.'

37

'Huh?' The man looked puzzled, and a little hurt.

'Don't you know,' she continued testily, 'that every authoritative text on criminology says that in poison-pen cases the guilty party has almost invariably later been proved to have sent one to himself and made a great to-do about it? That's the way their nasty little minds work; they think that it automatically clears them from suspicion. One of the people waiting inside your office is the murderer, or I miss my guess. Of course,' she added frankly, 'I have missed some important guesses in my time, but they say that even Homer nodded. Well, we might as well go inside, and start afresh from here.'

Cushak looked at her rather strangely, and the schoolteacher had a sense that he was now even more out of sympathy with her and her quest than he had been before. He was not, it appeared, used to having his decisions and actions questioned by underlings. But he shrugged, turned, and ushered her silently into his office.

She sniffed. She smell of fear was in that room. The three people who waited there were as jittery, she thought, as a cat on hot bricks. Miss Withers was introduced to them in strict studio seniority. First there was Jules Karas, music director—a man somewhere in his fifties, stocky and leonine and intensely masculine, who bowed stiffly from the waist and smoked thin cigars in a long amber holder. His eyes told her nothing at all; he had the practised aplomb of the European. A hard nut to crack, she thought.

Then there was Rollo Bayles, background artist. He was a pale, somewhat wispy man with a face that might have been handsome if the sculptor hadn't left the clay half-finished and unsmoothed. His hand, when Miss Withers grasped it, was dampish and thin—yet his nervous grip made her wince a little. A true introvert, she said to herself; a man, as the English say, with a *maggot*.

Last and far from least there was Janet Poole, a warmish, most generously-proportioned girl whose blue-violet eyes made one forget that she was plain—or was she really plain, after all? A young man, Miss Withers shrewdly decided, might have a difficult but no doubt most interesting time making up his mind about that. She liked the girl on sight —and at the same time she mistrusted her reaction, knowing full well that a person can smile and smile and be a villain still and that no one, not even herself, had the power to see the Mark of Cain.

'But I've seen her somewhere before,' the schoolteacher added to herself. 'Or else she looks like somebody in the movies. Darken that lovely hair and she'd be a dead ringer for Loretta Young.'

Then they got down to cases. None of the three admitted taking the poison-pen valentines very seriously, now that they had had a chance to think it over. Miss Withers's eyebrows went up, and she turned to Mr Cushak. 'You haven't told them yet?'

'Told them what?'

'Told them that Larry Reed has been murdered—and that somebody left one of the valentines in his office, which I just found!' She told them some of the details, and showed them the valentine.

The announcement fell heavily upon those in the office. Karas stiffened and Bayles quaked and Janet Poole tried to laugh and wound up almost crying. 'Us four!' she cried. 'One down and three to go.'

'Not necessarily,' pronounced the schoolteacher firmly. She turned to Karas. 'And just what was the content of your message?'

He hesitated, and drew a deep breath. 'Filth,' he said. 'It was all a lie.'

'What was, in particular?' Miss Withers asked reasonably.

'The nasty verse, which I do not remember. It intimates that I have abandoned by wife in the old country when the Russky swine take over, and that I make my escape leaving her to disappear and probably to die in a slave-labour camp in Siberia.'

'Your wife *Lucy*?'

Her name, he stoutly maintained, had been Anastasia.

39

He himself had been away in Italy on a concert tour when the Iron Curtain had clamped itself down on his unhappy homeland; because of his past political background it would have been sure death for him to go home. He had tried vainly through the Red Cross and all other possible sources to get word of her or to her. And he had never known anybody anywhere named Lucy and had no idea at all why that name should have been signed to the valentines.

Nor had either of the others ever known a Lucy, Miss Withers found out on further exploration. Rollo Bayles diffidently admitted that his valentine had been addressed 'To the Cowardly Apostate'—some fifteen years ago while still in his late teens he had briefly studied for the priesthood to please his mother, but had been more interested in art and other worldly affairs and on the gentle but firm advice of his superiors he had renounced his vocation before taking vows. 'But who would want to drag that up now?' he complained in a high, brittle voice. 'Who would even *know*?'

'Perhaps we deal with a mind-reader,' Miss Withers suggested drily. 'Or perhaps you let something slip in a careless moment of conversation; people often do. A friendly bartender, or something like that?'

Bayles slowly shook his head, but he frowned thoughtfully.

Janet Poole, next in line, was less cooperative. Her soft red mouth set itself firmly. 'Tell you or anybody else what was in my valentine? I think I'd rather die first.'

'The whole purpose of this meeting,' the schoolteacher reminded her, 'is to see that you don't die. Very well, we'll respect your privacy for the time being at least. And we'll have to skip the mysterious Lucy character for the nonce— though it would be most interesting to know if anyone of that name works here at the studio or ever did work here.' She looked inquiringly at Mr Cushak.

'I have already checked,' he admitted. 'She doesn't and she didn't. We had a Lurine and a Lucybelle and a Laverne, but no Lucy.'

'Really?' Miss Withers nodded thoughtfully. 'Then it

would appear that "Lucy" is the nom-de-plume of some-body else, perhaps even concealing the identity of a man, and that someone who knows you all and knows enough about you to stick a pin into a tender place has a most determined grudge. So who could it be?'

'Nobody!' said Jules Karas, spouting blue cigar smoke. 'Poppycock. I still think that somehow it is only a very bad joke.'

'A bad joke—with me stumbling on Larry Reed's body in his house up on Mulholland? I think not. Somebody has painted a target on you four people—and has already hit one bull's-eye.'

They seemed to shrink suddenly in upon themselves, but nobody said anything. The maiden schoolteacher looked severely at them. 'Just how often,' she asked quietly, 'have you four people worked together intimately?'

'But they haven't!' spoke up Ralph Cushak from behind his mahogany desk. 'This is a big studio, Miss Withers, with lots of different cartoon projects going on all the time. These four people may have had accidental contacts around the lot, and they certainly know one another to speak to, but to my knowledge they have never been assigned to the same story or worked together in the same office. Of course, Mr Karas here is in charge of all our music, assisted by such composers and musicians as he needs on a part-time basis. Mr Bayles paints the backgrounds for many of our pictures, especially those involving underwater scenes or woodland stuff. But Reed works—I mean worked—only on the Bird series, the Peter Penguin stuff, and Miss Poole here is animator on the Willy Wombat and Charley Chipmunk series, though now and then like all our people she sits in on a conference concerning one of the other characters. But these four people have had no regular contact, there is nothing whatever to link them together. The whole thing, if you ask me, is quite mad.'

'Almost too mad,' said Miss Withers slowly. 'Just why should a supposed homicidal maniac train his sights on these four? It's a sort of methodical nor'-nor'west madness

—the misquotation is from *Hamlet*, in case you're interested —and there's a link somewhere if we can only find it.' She pointed to the brown envelope addressed to Larry Reed. 'This drawing, and this printing—would you people say that they are the work of one of the regular studio artists?'

The thing was passed around again. They were of various opinions. The printing itself was sketchy and impersonal, of the type used by almost everyone in the place. Then when you came to the drawing of the murdered, strangled Bird—

'Was it drawn by a competent studio artist, or not?' Miss Withers demanded.

Nobody could immediately answer that. Of course, every desk in the place was equipped with a tracing-board designed to make it easy to reproduce the original gels—the master-drawings—with whatever minor changes of action were immediately indicated. Anyone in the place could, given time and access to one of the desks, have taken one of the myriad gelatine prints of Peter Penguin which overflowed the studio, tilted it horizontally and then traced it, adding his own ghoulish touches. This particular drawing, they agreed, was a trifle crude—but perhaps purposely so.

'Then it must have been done,' the schoolteacher decided wisely, 'by an amateur who was trying to draw like a professional or a professional who was trying to draw like an amateur, which gets us exactly nowhere.'

'Except that we know by the stationery and everything that it must have been done by somebody right here in the studio,' said Mr Cushak sadly. 'One of our own people has gone bad—'

'Like the rotten apple that must be nipped in the bud,' put in Miss Withers a bit wickedly. Again she stared at the three marked victims; if the books were right one of them was the murderer of Larry Reed. None of them looked at all like a murderer; of course she knew to her sorrow that murderers rarely did. Lombroso and his criminal types had long been discredited; the murderer often looked like and *was* the nice person next door who borrowed your lawnmower and lent you an egg or a cup of sugar when you were short. For once the schoolteacher had no intuition, no hunch, no touch of extrasensory perception to guide her. Yet she much inclined to the belief that two of these people in the office were honestly scared for their very lives and that one was a very fine actor and a deep-dyed villain.

'I suggest,' she said quietly, 'that for the next few days each one of you takes exceptional precautions; we are in the midst of something ugly and dangerous. And if any one of you should happen to remember anything about anyone named Lucy—' She nodded goodbye at them and made her way out and back to her own office, where she found Tip Brown pinning up new drawings on the story-board facing her desk. Talley erupted from his favourite spot in the corner and greeted her as if she had been away for a year; almost equally enthusiastic was Tip, whose face was boyishly alight.

'Hi!' he said. 'I think I got it. This story was originally developed too straight-line. It's gotta have a zany, Milt Gross touch—and your Talley dog suggests it. He had lunch with me, by the way. I hope it was all right.'

'I hope so too,' she said. 'One raw hamburger?'

'Two,' he admitted. 'And the beastie sat up and begged for more, so I bought him an ice-cream cone for dessert.'

'Talleyrand has gone Hollywood,' said the schoolteacher, shaking her head. 'He'll have to reduce—'

'Anyway, he's type-casting if ever. You see, we've got to wring out all the boffs and yaks we can from the situations where the circus poodle tries to ham it up and get into every act in the show and out-clown the clowns and out-fly the acrobats. I've got a swell idea for a sequence where he tries to take over and peddle toy gas balloons to the audience only he gets hold of too many and they lift him right up to the top of the big tent—'

'Splendid,' said Miss Withers absently. 'But—'

'And for a climax,' continued Tip Brown, 'we pull a switcheroo. The rich old lady in sequence one, she doesn't die after all, she gets better. There's publicity in the circus ads. about the poodle and back in the big house on Fifth

Avenue the parrot recognizes him—he's the type of parrot who always reads the morning paper, natch—and he flies out the window and comes over to the circus hell-bent to bring the good news and say hello to an old friend and tell the poodle that he can go home again, the relatives have been thrown out on their respective behinds. Only the pup doesn't go for it. Suddenly he realizes that he likes the circus better than the plush spot in the big house, and he doesn't want to go back. He's now a featured performer and the ringmaster has to treat him with respect and he's among friends. He'll stay here—and, he mentions, there happens to be an opening for a barker in the side-show—'

'I was thinking,' began Miss Withers hopefully, 'about—'

'So we dissolve to the parrot outside the side-show, yelling, "Hurry, hurry, hurry—get your tickets for the prime attraction of the midway . . ." or whatever it is. The parrot got into the act too, see? Happy ending, with the spotlight on the poodle in the centre ring of the circus, juggling something ten times his size and having a hell of a time. He's found himself; he's among friends, see?'

'I like it fine,' said the schoolteacher judicially. 'But speaking of friends, what about Larry Reed? What sort of person would you say he was?'

Tip looked vaguely puzzled. 'Larry? Good artist, full of fun and games. The type who would put itching powder in your bath-salts if he had a chance, or slip rubber sausages in the hors-d'œuvre. He used to pick up copies of cheap magazines and then spend hours filling in the advertising coupons with his friends' names, so that for months afterwards they'd have their mail-boxes stuffed with home-tattooing sets and patent remedies for baldness and lost manhood and stuff like that. Oh, Larry's a card.'

'And speaking of cards,' she pressed closer, 'did he win a lot from you and the boys at poker?'

'But—' Tip looked bewildered. 'He never played it. He did a lot of card tricks, he was even a member of the American Society of Magicians, but he said it wasn't fair

44

for him to compete across the table. I never knew him to gamble, except maybe a little on a Christmas Eve crap game or on a horse at Santa Anita. I thought he spent most of his evenings at the easel painting things; he was hell-bent on being a real artist and having exhibitions in New York and a spread in *Life*.'

'And what about the other evenings, when he didn't paint? Was he interested in women?'

Tip grinned. 'Who isn't? As the fellow said, "It's me hobby!" Yes, Larry gets around, but he never sticks to anyone long. I guess that's why Joyce pulled out and left him.'

'Was there much bitterness in that divorce?'

'None, that I know of. He had a sense of humour and she didn't. He used to carry a little gold bell, and ring it at her when there was a gag and she didn't get it, to show he was only kidding.'

'Any man who would ring a pocket bell at *me* . . .' said Miss Withers. 'But do go on.'

'There's not much more to it,' Tip Brown said. 'They just didn't fit, and there weren't any children to complicate things, so he gave her the car and the TV set and he took the house and they parted amicably—they still have dinner every now and then. Very modern and all that.'

'How charming,' said Miss Withers, without warmth. 'Is there anybody else whose toes Larry Reed might have stepped on?'

Tip Brown stared at her. 'Not that I know of. Larry's not the type to make a play for married women; there are enough luscious unattached young females around this town for anybody. They're mostly dying to get a studio job, and they cluster around anybody who works for a studio like flies around a garbage can.'

'I see,' said the schoolteacher. 'But didn't Larry make some enemies with his practical jokes?'

'Not really. Oh, he carried a sort of torch for Janet Poole, the blonde lovely here in the studio, after she turned him down for her musician. But leave it to Larry to get even in his own boyish fun-loving way—he knew this fellow had ambitions to be an actor, so he sent him a fake phone message supposedly coming from Sam Goldwyn's office asking him to come over for a screen-test. The poor guy pawns his watch to buy a new suit and then spends half a day at the Goldwyn Studio trying to get past the gatemen.'

'And so everybody took Larry Reed's jokes in good humour? You yourself, when he forwarded all your mail to Arizona?'

He stiffened. 'At that time I could cheerfully have strangled him, sure. But in this business you have to go along with a gag. Finally I saw the joke, and laughed as hard as any of them.'

Miss Withers had her own ideas about that, but she kept them to her maidenly bosom. 'Then Larry Reed must have had great personal charm, to be so readily forgiven for his fun-loving Rover-Boy tricks.'

'Wait a minute!' Tip's face was strange. 'I—I begin to get it. You've been talking about Larry in the past tense for the last half hour. He's dead, isn't he?'

'You don't seem especially surprised at that, young man.'

Bu he wasn't listening. 'Something's happened to Larry, and you know all about it—that's why you've been asking all these questions!'

'Yes. He was murdered by somebody in this studio. Statistics show that murder happens every twenty minutes in these United States. I ask you again, have you any idea who it could be?'

Tip Brown seemed perceptibly to withdraw within himself, like an alarmed turtle. He was suddenly all carapace, unreachable. 'No,' he said hollowly. 'No, no ideas at all.' Quickly he pinned up the rest of his sketches and then said that he guessed he would call it a day. He went out of the office with a vague farewell gesture which indicated to the schoolteacher that he would see her around some time but preferably not soon.

That young man, she thought, knows more than he is telling—and he has told more than he meant to tell.

46

Miss Withers sat alone—except for the somnolent Talley in his corner—for a long time in the little office which had so much to tell her if walls could only speak, which they never seemed to do. Finally she switched on the light under the glass of the drawing-board, inserted a gelatine of The Bird and a sheet of paper over it, and started experimenting. After a few minutes she decided that with these aids even she could produce a fairly recognizable sketch of Peter Penguin; certainly very nearly as good as the one on the poison-pen valentine. She fell into a light brown study, from which she was aroused by Talley's enthusiastic welcome of a visitor. The girl she knew as Janet Poole was standing in the doorway, looking uncertain and lost.

'May I see you for a moment?' Jan asked. 'I—I just thought of something.'

Janet came in and sat down, crossing a rather remarkable pair of legs. But she found it hard to talk. 'Well?' said the schoolteacher.

'A while ago in Mr Cushak's office you asked if there was anything to link the three of us—I mean the four of us if you count Larry Reed . . .'

'Speak up, young lady. What is it?'

The girl carefully pleated her tweed skirt. 'It couldn't of course have had anything to do with what happened to Larry, I'm sure of that. But I've been thinking it over, and I guess I ought to tell you. You see—when I first came to the studio a couple of years ago I—I went out sometimes with Larry. I went out with Rollo Bayles too—and even once or twice with Mr Karas, who may be old but has some young ideas. All the bachelors around the place give a new girl the rush, you know.'

'I wouldn't know, never having been in that happy situation. But you are trying to say that you played the field, eh?'

'A girl has to do something with her evenings,' said Janet defensively. 'I was living in a boarding-house and bored to tears.'

'Say no more, my dear. It's my life story in a nutshell. But do go on.'

47

'There was never anything actually romantic,' Jan protested almost too quickly. 'Mr Karas was very gallant and continental and awfully sweet, really. He taught me a lot about food and wines and he kissed my hand. That's all he ever kissed—I expected more and was all ready to say "No," but it stopped there; I'm sure that he's really in love with that lost wife of his. Rollo Bayles—well, Rollo is a lonely, confused sort of guy; I think he's never got over a sort of guilt complex about leaving the priesthood, though heaven knows he was no more fitted for it than I am to be a—steam-fitter. But he's a jazz fan and we used to go out to a little place on Ventura Boulevard and sit there and nurse our beers and listen to Pete Dailey and the other hot five-man combos . . .'

'I have heard them on the radio,' admitted the schoolteacher. 'They take tunes apart and put them back together sideways. But what about you and Larry Reed?'

'Larry was the nicest and most exciting of the lot, in most ways. But his divorce wasn't final then and I didn't want to get serious about a man who was at least technically married. We went dancing to Mocambo and Ciro's and places like that, but before the thing got really final . . .' The girl hesitated.

'And—' prompted Miss Withers.

'Before his divorce got final, something happened,' said Janet, a bit dreamily. 'But you must understand; we all stayed friends.'

'Somebody didn't stay just friends,' observed Miss Withers, nodding towards the diamond on Janet's ringfinger.

A warmish, crooked, little-girl smile illumined Jan's face. 'Guy,' she said softly. 'All this I'm telling you about happened before Guy came to stay at my boarding-house. He was a sorta lost guy, a crazy mixed-up kid as they say, but there was a piano in the place and I heard him play and suddenly I woke up and there I was—engaged to be married. It's going to be this summer.'

'You are referring to the musician, I gather?'

'Guy? Yes, he plays the piano and makes arrangements. But he's really a composer.'

'How nice,' said Miss Withers a bit absently. 'Musicians and artists—aren't they supposed to be the jealous type? Do you suppose there could possibly be the shade of a jealousy motive here?'

Janet laughed out loud. 'Heavens, no! Do I look like a *femme fatale*?'

'I wouldn't know,' said Miss Withers. 'Never having for obvious reasons been accused of it myself.' But all the same, the schoolteacher was wondering a little; there was something about this long tall blonde girl which could perhaps have been very disturbing to the right man—or the wrong man. 'Your fiancé works here at the studio?' she pressed.

'Guy? Why yes, when he works. He's a song-writer, and going to be one of the best. He wrote *Lullaby for a Pink Elephant*, a wonderful novelty number that's just been published in New York! This music arrangement thing he's doing here is fairly new to him, but he's always fooled around with the piano. He played at the boarding-house when he didn't know anybody was listening, and I grabbed hold of him and introduced him to Mr Karas, who gave him a job. Believe you me—' She smiled, her eyes clear and confident. 'Somebody just had to take over that boy and straighten him out; he has so much talent and ability. This music arrangement thing is just for now. Guy's finished two new songs—*Flitterbug Jump* and *Lady Bewitched*, and when they come out—' Her face was lighted up with a neon sign. 'Guy is really going places; his publishers says he's going to be another Cole Porter!'

'"I know where I'm going, and I know who's going with me . . ."' Miss Withers softly hummed the old Scottish ballad. 'How nice for you, my dear. Tell me, Miss Poole, just between us girls, what was in your poison-pen valentine to make you tear it up?'

Janet set her firm chin. 'I—I couldn't!'

'You *must*. And I promise it won't go any farther.'

'It—it was just something dirty and unfair! It brought up my one dark secret. You see, years ago when I was an art student at Otis here in Los Angeles I had to work most of my way. My father is only a steam-fitter down in Long Beach and he couldn't always pay the rent on time at home and buy the groceries, much less help me in what I laughingly call my career. If you must know, I—I did some posing for the life classes at art school, that's all. In the nude.' She swallowed. 'I thought I'd lived it down, but—'

'It has never seemed to me,' interposed the schoolteacher, 'that there is anything evil about the human body—especially a body like yours—unless thinking makes it so. It shouldn't make any difference to your young man—'

'It didn't!' Janet flashed. 'I told Guy, of course, and he never batted an eye. But if it ever got back to his snooty family in Hartford, don't you see? There'd never be a chance in the world of their accepting him and his bride.' She shuddered. 'Not that it especially matters to me, but it matters so much to him. He wants me to walk into the family mansion like a fairy princess . . .'

'Most men do. But let us get down to cases. Who else could know about this deep dark secret of yours?'

'But *nobody*!' Janet insisted. 'It all happened years ago, when I was a green kid from the wrong side of the tracks and before I changed my name; it was Janiska Pazky then, believe it or not.'

'I can believe it easily,' said the schoolteacher. 'Poole is easier to spell than Pazky. What else is the melting-pot for? We are all descended from parents who got tired of their homelands and came here to do it differently, and many of them simplified their names. My great-great-grandfather was named Witherspoon, by the way; somewhere along the line the spoon got lost. So I wouldn't take it too seriously. And I wouldn't worry too much about your young man's family finding out about your having posed for an art-class of fellow-students; there's nothing dishonourable in that. But speaking of posing—just when did you pose for Larry Reed, or sit for him?'

50

Janet looked blankly innocent. 'Never, of course!'

The schoolteacher nodded noncommitally, remembering the unfinished watercolour on the dead man's easel. Now she remembered why Jan's face had looked so familiar on their first meeting in Mr Cushak's office. But, as she also knew, the innocent could lie as well as the guilty. 'I still suggest, young lady, that you lock your door and windows tonight, and that if you get a box of gift candy or anything else in the mail, you don't eat any of it.'

'But nobody ever sends me anything,' Janet confessed. 'The Hollywood swains never give out with anything but their time. And besides, everybody knows I'm bespoke. As us Polacks say—I been *friending around wit'* Guy for over a year.' She smiled a dreamish smile. 'And he's not one for presents, either. He's saving his money for a very important purpose. Oh, maybe a rose on my birthday . . .'

'Always one perfect rose—never one perfect Cadillac,' quoted Miss Withers. 'I know. All the same, my dear, I think that extra precautions are indicated for you. Those valentines aren't in the pure spirit of fun, you know.'

Janet nodded slowly. 'I *do* know. But I still can't really believe it, somehow. Nobody in the studio would do a thing like that, nobody at all. If they get mad at somebody they think it over and then pull a gag, a practical joke, and let it go at that. This—this sort of thing is evil and mean!'

'It is indeed. But—'

'Oh, heavens!' Janet had looked at her watch. 'My man's waiting at the gate.'

'Never keep them waiting,' advised the schoolteacher. 'At least not very long. I lost one that way.'

But the girl had already sailed out of the door. Something impelled Miss Withers to shadow her and see this shining young man of hers, but the phone suddenly came alive. It was Mr Cushak.

'Miss Withers? Put your mind at rest,' said the studio executive. 'I have good news. It's all just a false alarm!'

'What?' she gasped indignantly.

'Reed's death was natural, or at least accidental, according to the Los Angeles county coroner's office. They just reported that he died from the effects of poison-ivy.'

'Stuff and nonsense,' said Miss Withers, but she said it under her breath.

CHAPTER 4

'Death stretched out his long hand towards the delicate little flower . . .'
— HANS CHRISTIAN ANDERSEN

It was all on page three of the early edition of tomorrow's *Times* out that evening. Lawrence Reed, 36, studio cartoonist, had been found dead in his home on Mulholland Drive, the victim—according to the coroner's office—of acute poison-ivy poisoning. Investigation by the police had shown that the weed grew profusely on parts of his canyon property, and it was thought by authorities that, not knowing himself to be abnormally susceptible to poison-ivy, Reed had inadvertently chewed on a twig of it while working around the place . . .

'Stuff and nonsense again,' said Miss Withers to the poodle. 'That doesn't explain anything; it's just a convenient cover-up. Reed hadn't been gardening; he was all dressed up and had just got home from the studio. He parked his car hastily in the flower-beds and rushed inside, leaving his keys in the dashboard, indicating that he was very ill.' She nodded to herself and then put through a long-distance call to New York City; it was a time for action and she needed all the help she could get. All the circuits were at the moment busy of course, but she had barely finished making a frugal supper for herself and opening a can of horse-meat for Talley when the bell rang—not the phone as she had hoped, but the door-bell.

'Who on earth—?' she said. She opened the door and found that it was Janet Poole.

52

'Excuse me—I mean us—for disturbing you,' the girl was saying in the doorway. And then the schoolteacher saw that close behind her was a tall, palely-handsome young man who must obviously be her musician; he looked just as a pianist-composer should look, only perhaps with a neater haircut and more expensive if well-worn clothes. Yes, Janet introduced him as her fiancé, Guy Fowler, somewhat pridefully. 'We're here because Guy put his foot down and insisted. There's maybe something you ought to know.'

'There are many things I ought to know,' admitted Miss Withers ruefully. 'Most of which I don't.' She found them chairs and ashtrays, forcibly cut short the poodle's usual fanfare of welcome, and settled herself down. 'Well?'

Jan looked at her young man for comfort, evidently found it, and plunged on in. 'You must understand—this was something I had completely forgotten. I don't see what it could have had to do with the valentines, but—well, about a year ago the studio decided to preview a cartoon feature and three short subjects out at Santa Ana, down in the orange country. Of course, everybody who'd worked on the pictures wanted to see the preview, but the studio staff cars were all busy so they sent some of us down in rented limousines. Just as it happened, Mr Karas, Rollo Bayles, Larry Reed and I all went in one. I'd forgotten about it, but Guy reminded me at dinner tonight.'

'Yes,' Guy Fowler said, very serious. 'I'm naturally most disturbed,' he admitted in a faint Ivy-League accent. 'From what Jan tells me, there's supposed to be a mysterious link between those four people. I'm fairly a newcomer here, but it occurred to me that that was one time the four were together, it that's worth anything to you.'

'I don't see—' began Miss Withers, slightly puzzled.

'We were together by purest accident,' Jan cut in hurriedly. 'In this car from the limousine service. It was a perfectly horrible night for driving, one of those impossible deluges we have sometimes during the rainy season, and even the birds were walking. Down in some dismal street in south-east Los Angeles the driver had an accident. He hit a woman who ran out in front of him, against the lights, to catch a bus. We saw nothing of it, just felt the thud and heard a scream. The driver stopped and an ambulance came. The police asked a lot of questions, but they didn't even hold him. We went on to the preview and the woman was taken away to a hospital and lingered on and on and I guess maybe later she died though there was nothing much about her in the papers. But do you suppose, maybe—?'

'I can suppose anything,' said the schoolteacher. 'But perhaps it is something to think about.'

Guy Fowler absently ashed his cigarette in the pot where Miss Withers's precious African violets were growing. 'I'm just wondering,' he said. 'Suppose the woman who was hit had a boyfriend who was knocked off his rocker by the shock of her death, and set out to get even?'

The schoolteacher sniffed a prodigious sniff. 'Come, come, young man! A boyfriend who'd get a job at the studio with intent to murder all the people who just happened to be passengers in the car that struck her? It sounds rather far-fetched to me at first glance, though I'll confess that in my humble opinion there is never a really sufficient motive for murder. But it will stand looking into, I suppose. Was the woman's name Lucy, by any chance?'

Jan shook her head. 'I don't know. Maybe.'

'I'll find out. We have to pursue every avenue and every blind-alley. Because in spite of what it says in the newspapers, Larry Reed was murdered by the sender of those Lucy valentines.'

'But,' cried Jan, bewildered, 'he died of poison-ivy!'

'And I think,' observed the schoolteacher quietly, 'that that will stand looking into too; there have been wrong diagnoses before this.'

'Well, whether it's wrong or whether it's right,' the young man said almost belligerently, 'I'm not going to have Jan left on a spot. Something drastic has to be done about it, right now. I wish the studio would call in a regular private agency like Burns or Pinkerton . . .'

'Guy dear!' Janet interrupted. 'Please hush!'

He subsided, a bit sulkily. 'She bosses him a little,' Miss Withers said to herself. But she'd learn, if she were wise. The schoolteacher pondered for a moment. 'I have a suggestion. You two could get married and go off somewhere on a honeymoon right away, far out of danger.'

There was a stiffish silence. Then Janet, fumbling in her handbag briefly, said, 'Guy darling, will you run out and see if I left my cigarettes in the glove compartment?'

He started to offer her his own cigarette case, but she shook her head. 'You know I can't stand those king-sized things of yours.'

'Certainly.' Guy gave her a look and then excused himself with easy politeness and went out the door, followed by Jan's fondly-possessive glance and also by Talley the poodle, who was tired of all this conversation and thought it was time for a breather.

Alone with the girl Miss Withers said, 'My dear, you must forgive me if I have touched on a tender subject or something, but it did seem an eminently sensible idea under the present circumstances. Eloping, I mean.'

Janet Poole frowned. 'Since you know this much, you might as well know the rest of it. Guy and I are going to get married as soon as we can, but he's a dear foolish idealist and so he stubbornly says that he won't make an honest woman of me until he pays back every cent of the money he had to borrow from me while he was on his uppers.' The girl leaned confidentially closer, her eyes warmly maternal. 'You see, when I first met Guy he'd been having a rough time of it. His family back east had more of less thrown him out on his ear because he wouldn't toe the line, get his degree from Yale or Harvard and come into the firm— they're investment counsellors or something like that, and have been since Plymouth Rock was a pebble. He had a brief unhappy marriage that they arranged—to a high-nosed, icy society deb next door; she got a Paris divorce. Everything went wrong for Guy, with too much bossing from her and from his parents. He'd drifted out here to Hollywood and was trying to be an actor, without getting anywhere. He'd been trying to be a writer too—he did literally dozens of stories in the hard-boiled detective field and also some science-fiction, but he never sold anything. He was drinking too much and going to hell in a handbasket if you'll pardon my French. But he moved into my rooming-house, and that time I heard him play the piano I knew right away that he had something, even if he'd never been able to find it. So—'

'So you took over? Most men can stand a little intelligent guidance, I've heard. None of them would stand still long enough for me to try, darn it. But it's not a bad basis for marriage, either. You've never met this family of his?'

Janet shivered. 'No, but I will this summer. I'll be terribly nice and refined, too. That's why I'm studying speech and Emily Post so I won't look to them just like a green Polack from south of the tracks, or pick up the wrong fork. Because—' the girl hesitated—'you see, while Guy is now estranged from his family he's terribly in awe of them and I know he'd never be happy for long without their approval of his marriage. Now that he's found himself and becoming a different person and stopped drinking, now that he's starting out to be a successful composer and another Cole Porter, maybe—'

'It should certainly make a difference in their attitude, and I hope they will see clearly enough to give you credit for the transformation. And has he met *your* family?'

Janet's smile was glowing and proud. 'Of course! And he did *beautiful*. He went down to Long Beach with me one week-end; he ate my mamma's *bigos* and *kielbasa* and drank a couple of puddlers—that's the Polish name for boiler-makers—with my pop. Guy took it all in his stride; he didn't even seem to mind Pop sitting around the kitchen in his undershirt. He did disappoint my brother by refusing to go out in the back yard and wrestle, but he beat him at chess. It all went off better than we'd even dared hope; they seemed to like him really. But of course anything I do is okay with my family; I could marry King Kong and if he had a regular job and didn't beat me too often they'd give their blessing.'

Miss Withers nodded, feeling that she too would be inclined to trust this long, tall, open girl. But of course, she reminded herself, you couldn't trust anybody at this stage of a murder case. 'So far so good, then,' she said cautiously. 'Is your Guy the jealous type?'

'*Him?*' With quick understanding, Janet said firmly, 'Don't think what I think you're thinking. Guy isn't at all the jealous type; he was never jealous of Larry Reed or anybody I went out with before he came into my life. He's got reasons to know there was never any important men for me and that I'm all his, period.'

'Period and exclamation point, eh?' The schoolteacher. was inclined to believe her. These one-man women, and how well she understood them! 'Sorry, but in this business we have to ask all sorts of questions. When there's a murder, and the threat of three more, everyone is in a way suspect. I confess that I do not at the moment see a plausible motive for anybody's killing Larry Reed, but—'

'Larry Reed was a sweet guy!' Janet protested. 'A sorta wolf, but a sweet guy. Just because he pulled some practical jokes—'

'Practical jokes can cut rather deeply sometimes,' Miss Withers reminded her. 'How about Tip Brown. Didn't he have a feud with Reed?'

'Tip?' Janet laughed. 'He's a sweet guy, the second sweetest I know. He's the sort of person who feeds the mice around his apartment, and climbs trees to put baby robins back in the nest when they fall out. I'd love Tip a little, I guess, if I wasn't so very bespoke.'

'An excellent attitude, but—' began Miss Withers, and then looked up to see Guy Fowler returning, complete with unnecessary cigarettes and the waltzing poodle, who made it clear that he had adopted Guy as a foster-father.

'It's cold outside,' Guy apologized. 'I walked your dog down to the corner, but he wanted to go seventeen blocks at double-pace and I'm not in condition. You girls are maybe through discussing me?'

57

Janet shook her head warningly at him, and he subsided into a chair. Miss Withers said, somewhat tactfully, 'We are about through discussing everything at the moment, young man. Take that small chip off your shoulder—I am quite as interested in protecting your fiancée as you are, and just possibly in some ways better equipped. The fact remains that she has been threatened with one of these stupid but deadly valentines, and that it behoves you of all people to keep a close eye on her.'

Slightly chastened, the young man promised faithfully that Janet would be locked in her room within the hour.

'Fine. But most murders seem to take place in locked rooms,' the schoolteacher murmured.

'That's it!' Janet cried. 'Let us forget all about this stuff tonight, and go lose ourselves in a crowd. Mocambo, maybe?' She did a rhumba step.

'Barney's Beanery is just as crowded and a good deal cheaper,' Guy Fowler said.

'But yesterday was pay-day—'

'Yesterday was *your* pay-day,' the young man patiently reminded her. 'Not mine. I have made exactly forty-eight dollars this week, and spent sixty of it. Would you settle for a drive-in movie, maybe?'

'"Always one perfect rose . . ."' Jan quoted. But the schoolteacher envied the trusting way the girl took Guy's arm as they went out and down the steps and across the lawn to the modest black sedan of elderly vintage which waited there. She also envied the way the girl was tenderly ushered into the car behind the wheel, and wished that just once Oscar Piper would remember to open doors for her.

After the young couple had left, the room was very silent, very filled with question-marks. Miss Withers was thinking of washing her hair or taking another bath—her very last expedients when things refused to happen—but the New York call came through a few minutes after eleven. The voice of her old friend and ally the Inspector, skipper of Manhattan's homicide bureau, was a bit on the testy side.

58

'Hildegarde,' he said, 'do you happen to know what time it is back here?'

'I am much too busy, Oscar, to play guessing games. You got me into this—'

'Into what? Oh, the funny valentine thing at the cartoon studio. Yeah, I met this guy who's at the head of it—Mantz or Lantz or something like that, a cheery soul—at one of our special meetings of the Third Avenue Schooner and Pastrami Club, and beat him a few hands of stud. Somehow we got to talking and he said he had a problem and I mentioned your name and gave you a recommend. Nothing to it, I suppose?'

'Nothing, Oscar, but one corpse—which I discovered after a bit of house-breaking. One down and three to go.'

'Judas priest in a handbasket!' Oscar Piper came wide awake. 'What in—'

'Oscar, please listen. This is running into money, and I'm not sure if I have an expense account or not. I just called to ask you if ever in your wide professional experience you'd heard of a murder being committed with poison-ivy?'

In the long silence which ensued, she could clearly hear the scratch of a match at the other end of the line. 'Oscar, if you have your cheroot lighted now,' the schoolteacher said tartly, 'I'll repeat the question. Can poison-ivy kill?' She waited, tapping her front teeth with a long, unvarnished fingernail. 'You there?'

'Yes,' the Inspector finally said, in a very odd tone. 'Yes, to both questions. I was just floored for a minute. '"The *weed of hell*" as some poet called it,' she interposed.

'It's generally supposed to be poisonous but not deadly to the human system, but we had a case here, three-four years ago—one that's always rankled in my craw. A night club dancer named Zelda Bard or Ward or something like that got an anonymous bottle of brandy in the mail as a Christmas present and died a short time after from what Doc Bloom, our medical examiner, said was a concentrated extract of poison-ivy or poison-oak—both the same damn' thing. She must have been very susceptible, for she was swelled up like—like—'

'Like a poisoned pup?' Miss Withers said gently. 'Mine *too*.'

'Sweet spirits of nitre!' Oscar Piper cried. 'This can't be just coincidence. That same killer must be at work again out there!'

'It could be,' admitted the schoolteacher. 'What next, Oscar?'

He thought about it. 'And I had to go and get you into a thing like that,' he said ruefully, with real worry in his voice. 'Poisoners are the worst of all, because they're sneaky. This is mean stuff, a good deal out of your class, and you might easily get hurt. I think—' He hesitated again.

'*You* think? Are you really equipped for it, Oscar?'

'Stop trying to be funny. I was about to say that I think I can talk the Commish into okaying a trip west for me, since he is as anxious as I am to get to the bottom of the Bard case. I'll take the next plane for Los Angeles and straighten out the whole thing for you. Meanwhile, do nothing until I get there, understand?'

'I understand, but do not agree,' said the schoolteacher with her usual firmness. 'You don't see the entire situation, Oscar. I am in the midst of a series of four murders, one down and three to go as I told you. The time to solve a murder is before it happens. But of course I'll be glad to have your help if they let you off the hook. Wire me when to meet you.'

Remembering her driving, Oscar Piper said hastily, 'No thanks, Hildegarde. I'll not trouble you to drive all that distance. I can take a taxi from the airport.'

She sniffed again. 'Very well. Good night, Oscar. And for heaven's sake remember to put out that cigar before you go back to bed, for your own safety.' She hung up, feeling slightly encouraged about it all; poison-ivy had been used at least once as a method of murder. And murderers, as she knew from most bitter experience, had a tendency to repeat themselves until caught; it was like that first salted peanut.

60

But there was also the story of the pitcher which went once too often to the front . . .

Miss Hildegarde Withers gave her greying hair its requisite one hundred strokes and then sought her maidenly couch, hoping that in her sleep her subconscious mind would come up with a hint or two about the problem which plagued her. She slept—finally—but her dreams were only a photo-montage of cracked pitchers and half-done water-colours, of clowning poodles floating from balloons and bottles of mineral oil and shoes and ships and sealing-wax, all to the accompaniment of the tuneless, maniacal laughter of a dying penguin . . .

Back in New York City Inspector Oscar Piper, one of the three people who could get the police commissioner up out of bed at this hour, did so. 'I'm going out to California,' he said.

'Huh?' The commissioner was still half asleep. 'Okay, but why?'

'Zelda Bard.'

'She's there? Oh no, she's dead, isn't she. You got something?'

'Hildegarde Withers has. I threw a case to her, just to keep her from brooding, and it turns out to be something. Same deal—the poison-ivy stuff. I don't mind these murders we get with knives and guns, but when they start using new stuff—'

'Exactly.' The commissioner was wide awake now. 'Go ahead. Swarthout can take over your office while you're gone. You want a plane?'

The air-wing of the New York police department consists of two Bell D-47 helicopters, capable of no more than a modest 100 miles an hour with favourable winds. 'No thanks,' said Piper hastily. 'I'll go by regular air line— I've gotta get out there before Hildegarde gets herself into trouble. But I'm fairly sure that he's at work again out there in California . . .'

'He?' said the commissioner.

'Maybe *she*. Zelda Bard could have been killed by a

jealous rival, but I always had a hunch it was one of her multitudinous boyfriends who sent her the poison-ivy brandy. We'll see.'

'Okay, Oscar. Take all the time you need—take two or three days if necessary.'

'Thank you, sir,' said the Inspector, and hung up. He looked ruefully and wistfully at the rumpled bed in which he had had only a couple of hours, and then got on the phone to arrange plane passage and money. He had eight dollars in his wallet, and he remembered the old story— California is the land of gold, and you'd better bring the gold with you.

There was finally a friendly bartender on Third Avenue who thought he could dig up a quick $500 . . .

Back on the lower left-hand corner of the nation, Miss Hildegarde Withers awoke at dawn, feeling somewhat like a worn-out dish-rag and very disappointed with her dreams; it was so often true that the watched subconscious never boils. She had an increasing feeling that somehow she had been manœuvred into playing somebody else's game with somebody else's rules.

A worthy antagonist—if this were only a battle of wits. But four people had been promised death, and one of them had received it. Somebody was playing for keeps. Over her breakfast coffee the maiden schoolteacher made a sudden decision; she would play hookey from the studio today. Her quarry lay there, but she had a feeling that the mystery would be solved, if at all, from a completely different angle.

There had been a woman who had died under the wheels of a rented limousine—or what amounted to the same thing, though it had taken weeks to make an end to that grim cycle. Perhaps it was too late to ask questions, but Miss Withers was determined to ask them all the same. She dressed herself in a conservative blue serge suit and donned a hat which the Inspector had once said reminded him of an abandoned owl's nest; she locked Talleyrand in the patio with a pan of water and some dog-biscuits and took off. A

62

moment later she took back again, to write a note and pin it to the door.

Inspector Oscar Piper, slightly pale around the gills from a fast and bumpy plane trip across the country and from an almost equally fast and bumpy taxi-ride into Hollywood from the Los Angeles municipal airport, found the note at around eight o'clock that evening. The grizzled little Hibernian read it by the flickering light of a match, bit through his ever-present cigar, and read it again. 'Oscar, the key is under the mat. If I'm not back when you get here, look for me at the Morgue.'

CHAPTER 5

'Savage I was sitting in my house, late, lone . . .'
—BROWNING

Oscar Piper did a double-take, spat out his cigar, and then —knowing Hildegarde of old—he sighed and bent down and found the key, then went inside. Turning on the lights, he suddenly was reminded that he was not alone; the worried bewhiskered face of Talleyrand the poodle appeared in the pane of the patio door, emitting plaintive sounds. The Inspector let the dog in, shook hands and paws half a dozen times, then finally managed to get loose and find the phone directory. He drew a deep breath when he discovered that Hildegarde had been at the Morgue—and evidently made somewhat of an impression on the attendants, as was only be be expected—but had not remained there permanently on one of the marble slabs.

He plunked himself down in an easy chair, lighted a fresh perfecto, and took out the file on the Zelda Bard case. It had been a very special murder, and one in which for various reasons he had a very special interest; not very many victims of homicide had been so beautiful or had lived so fully or died so terribly. There was a long list of her boyfriends, the potential suspects, all of whom had been more or less cleared. That lady had certainly got around . . .

Miss Withers returned home somewhat after nine, to find the Inspector and Talley both sound asleep, the dog upside down on the couch and Oscar sprawled uncomfortably in the chair, snoring gently. 'Well!' the schoolteacher observed tartly. 'Men sleep while women work; so runs the world away. Hello, Oscar.'

He sat up, blinking. 'Huh? Oh, hello. What have you been up to until this hour—riding your broomstick around the rooftops?'

'I've been up to plenty.' She came closer and observed him critically. 'Oscar, you need a haircut. You also need some hair on top.'

'I also need a new lead on the Bard case,' he said soberly. 'Maybe just through blind luck you've stumbled on it. Got anything new today?'

She hesitated. 'Perhaps. I don't quite know. This is a crazy mixed-up case. But I'll tell you about it after I give this ravening hound his dinner.'

'You might make mine the same,' said Oscar Piper hopefully. 'Up to now I have eaten six sticks of chewing gum today.'

Some time later, over a plate of scrambled eggs with chicken livers, he said, 'So far there's actually nothing to link the two cases except the poison, which is rare enough to make it all very interesting. Your case out here seems to come down to a matter of motive. We can eliminate one thing—your Larry Reed *wasn't* killed out of revenge for one of his so-called practical jokes; you just don't poison a man because he leaves a wheelbarrow full of water in your car.'

'Practical jokes—a misnomer, Oscar, if there ever was one . . . as I've said before. But I suppose you have a point —unless one of his stunts backfired and really hurt someone, of which we have no direct evidence.' She rose. 'More coffee?'

'You might just warm it up a little,' he said as he handed

her an empty cup. 'But to get back to cases. I'm interested in this Lucy angle.'

The schoolteacher nodded. 'Yes, Lucy. "She lived unknown, and few could know when Lucy ceased to be; but she is in her grave, and oh, the difference to me." Wordsworth.'

'The difference to *her*, you mean. Did you actually get on her trail?'

'That I did. And it's a most tantalizing thing.' Miss Withers shook her head dubiously, then produced her notebook. 'Full name Lucinda May Wersbeck, also known professionally as Lucy LeMay, white well-nourished female aged about 34, was struck by a sedan owned by the Hollywood Limousine Rental Service and operated by one Arthur Johnson, age 22. The accident took place on the corner of Orient Boulevard and 16th Place in the midst of a howling rainstorm at seven-thirty on the evening of January 14th a year and more ago. Witnesses said that the accident was unavoidable.'

'*All* accidents are unavoidable,' pronounced the Inspector, officially.

'Anyway, she was admitted to the emergency ward of the County Hospital at 7.55 on that night—with internal injuries and multiple fractures; she lingered on and finally managed to die there on February 11th.'

'Well!' said Oscar Piper. 'Now maybe we're getting somewhere.'

'Now maybe we're getting nowhere,' Miss Withers corrected. 'Lucy was by profession a B-girl and taxi-dancer; hardly the type of girl to arouse the grand passion in the hearts of men except perhaps temporarily in lonely sailors. She had presumably had a prime, but she was well past it. Who on earth would want to avenge her accidental death a year and more later after it happened—and not on the driver who killed her, but on the passengers? It just doesn't make sense, any way you look at it. And all the time she was in the hospital she never had a visitor, a bouquet, or even a phone call inquiring about her condition; I checked it with the office.'

The Inspector carefully set his cigar alight again. 'Maybe her boyfriend didn't know—?'

'Stuff and nonsense. Anybody who wanted Lucy could have located her with one phone call. That's the puzzle— why should somebody wait so long to avenge her, if that was the motivation at all, which I somehow wonder at?'

'He was out of town, out of the country. In the Army, maybe. Came back a year later and went off his trolley—'

'He must have gone off his trolley, as you put it, long before. Because Lucy was no rose, nor any violet by a mossy stone, either. On the contrary.'

'She was pretty, though?'

Miss Withers sniffed. 'Perhaps in her day, but not recently at any rate—though the records show that years ago she worked off and on in the movies as an extra—a dress-extra, wearing evening gowns and supplying atmosphere for night-club scenes with a champagne glass full of fizz-water in her hand. She never got up to the point where a director would let her read a line. More recently she had made a precarious living up and down Main Street, the Skid Row of this town, presumably working at the oldest profession— though she never was convicted of it. I talked to one of the nurses who attended her after the accident, and she confidentially told me that Lucy could best be described as having a face like a meat-axe with a fright-wig on top. Oscar, how on earth could a woman like that have any friend, relative or lover who would set out more than a year later to avenge her accidental death by trying to kill off all the people who happened to be riding in the car that struck her?'

'Yeah,' he said slowly. 'You got a point. You'd think if anybody did go out for revenge he'd aim at the driver.'

'Do you think I'd neglect that most obvious angle? Arthur Johnson left the limousine company last November to accept —in the words of the old joke—a very important position as private in the United States Army. He is now in Korea, but I checked with his parents and up until the time he left at least nobody seems to have made any threats against him.'

Oscar Piper thought about it. 'Maybe Mr X only got back to Los Angeles recently and learned what happened to Lucy last year?'

'Yes, Oscar. A possibility. But this afternoon I also made a trip out to Forest Lawn in Glendale and found that I was the first visitor there to do homage to Lucinda Wersbeck since her interment. Wouldn't you think that anyone interested enough to commit murder for her memory would at least first have made a pilgrimage to carry a bouquet of flowers to her grave?'

He said nothing, pointedly.

'Oscar, I said—wouldn't you think—?'

'Sometimes I do,' the Inspector said slowly. 'Forest Lawn, is it?' He leaned back and blew one smoke ring through another, a faint smile on his face. 'Yes,' Oscar Piper continued thoughtfully, 'this murder is a complicated business; you can't really expect anyone foolish enough to risk his life committing a murder to act reasonably about anything, except perhaps through some twisted logic of his own. But catching a murderer is somewhat like training a dog; the first rule is that you have to be smarter than they are.'

'How true,' Miss Withers nodded wryly, with a side glance towards the sleeping poodle. 'Sometimes with Talleyrand I'm inclined to wonder who's training whom.' She looked at the watch she wore, a watch that had been her mother's—a maidenly watch pinned to her maidenly bosom. 'At any rate, sufficient to the day is the evil thereof, and we have discussed enough evil for now. It's late. You're staying here, of course. You can share the spare room with Talley, who won't mind at all.'

'But I'd planned to go to a hotel—' he protested.

'Nonsense. If he snores, just hit him with a pillow or something. Besides, I'd rather like some protection around the house, the way things have been going. Do you mind? I don't think I'll be at all compromised, if that's what you're worrying about.'

So it was that the Inspector somewhat unwillingly bedded down on a flouncy feminine bed in the front bedroom of

Miss Withers's little rented bungalow that night. He slept fitfully, unused to the setting and also unused to the weight of a forty-pound French poodle spread lovingly across his feet. It was therefore not until very, very late that the weary little Hibernian really got a stranglehold on Morpheus—and even that hold was rudely broken about 2 a.m. when something came smashing through the window and the venetian blind to thud against his bed.

He woke instantly, groping blindly for the unaccustomed lamp—and heard the sound of a car motor racing away. Talley, startled out of doggish dreams, added little or nothing to the situation by bursting into a frenzy of barking. By the time Oscar Piper found the light, Miss Hildegarde Withers was in the doorway, an apparition in a grey flannel bathrobe and with her hair in incredible braids. She surveyed them with disfavour. 'You might try to be a little more quiet, you two!' she was saying.

'Look,' he said, pointing.

Then she saw the wrecked window, and what lay on the floor. 'Whatever in the world,' she gasped, 'has been going on?'

They saw it together—it was a small plaster statuette of an engaging penguin in evening clothes and yellow shoes—a fantastic, cartoon-world penguin with a noose of string about its throat to which was tied a folded note in the shape of a heart, a valentine. They read the valentine, unbelieving . . .

'TO THE SHARP-NOSED SNOOP:
    TAKE IT EASY, TAKE IT SLOW,
    ONE IS DOWN AND THREE TO GO,
    IF YOU'VE GOT TO MESS AROUND
    YOU WILL SOON BE UNDERGROUND
        WITH LUCY.'

'The nerve of him!' cried Miss Withers, in considerable indignation.

The Inspector managed to be official, even in his gaudy

pyjamas. 'Very significant,' he pronounced sagely. 'We know now that Lucy is not the sender of these valentines, since this admits she is dead. And we also know that the murderer is worried. Once you've got 'em off balance the battle is half over. But what's with the duck?'

Miss Withers studied the plaster image. 'It's not a duck, Oscar. It's a figurine of Peter Penguin, who is the sacred Bird around the studio; he plays the lead in most of the feature pictures. There was a drawing of him dead in the other valentines; now he's in three-dimensions. An attempt to scare me off, and a rather childish one.' She frowned. 'Unless it's all part of a pattern of simulated idiocy . . .'

The Inspector yawned, shivered, and pointedly climbed back between the sheets. 'Pattern-schmattern,' he said. 'Let's get some sleep.'

'Sleep? "Macbeth hath murdered sleep!" Shakespeare.'

'Oh, go back to bed, Hildegarde, and I'll have this thing solved for you by some time tomorrow.'

She stared at him. 'Oscar Piper, you sound awfully confident. What do you know that I don't?'

'Not too much, about this end of the case,' he said wearily. 'Only that you just muffed one essential clue, that's all. The difference between the talented amateur and the seasoned pro, that's all. I'll gladly bet you a week's pay—'

'I'm opposed as you know to gambling in all forms,' the schoolteacher said stiffly. 'Besides, I'm not at all sure that you're not right; at the moment this case is a complete puzzle to me. Mr X is obviously somebody inside the cartoon studio—yet nobody there could possibly descend to this level; they're all just crazy in a nice pixie-ish sort of way. These valentines—' She shook her head and moved towards the doorway, then turned back to say—a little wistfully— 'Oscar?'

'Yes, Hildegarde. What is it now?'

'Oscar, it just occurred to me. This is the first valentine I've received since I left high school—and it had to be a left-handed one!'

CHAPTER 6

*'. . . a tissue of absurd mistakes, arising from the confusion of
the different characters one with another . . .'*

—HAZLITT

The long, tall blonde in the cherry-red robe came striding
like a Valkyrie along the hall of the boarding-house, armed
with soap and towel. Her eyes were full of sleep, but she
looked determined and resolute and about 16 years old. She
paused to put her ear to a mighty oaken door and then
entered without knocking, closing it carefully behind her.

She crossed quickly to the tumble of blankets on the
bed, sought for and found a masculine face, and kissed it
enthusiastically. 'Awake!' cried Janet Poole cheerfully.
'"Awake, for morning in the bowl of night has flung the
stone that puts the stars to flight . . ." That's Fitzgerald.'

'Wau-ugh?' Guy Fowler muttered, and turned over.

She sat down on the edge of the bed, rumpling his hair
—not that it needed it. '"And lo! the hunter of the east has
caught the sultan's turret in a noose of light." See how I
remember?'

Guy grunted again.

'I like Fitzgerald,' she confessed. 'Not as much as Shakespeare, but I still like him—even if Fitz means descended
from an illegitimate son. Why aren't there any *Mac*Geralds,
huh?'

He sat up a little. 'Probably because the original Gerald
had only bastards, and you're another one for waking me up.'

She kissed him again. 'There! That's supposed to wake
any Sleeping Beauty. Though you'd look more like one if
you'd shave and comb your hair, darling. Come, it's almost
eight.'

'Thanks for the time-signal. Now please go 'way; I want
to sleep some more. I was up late last night.' He caught her

70

swift, worried look at the wastebasket. 'No, no empties there. I promised you, didn't I? And haven't I kept my promise for months?' He looked hurt. 'I was working.' Guy gestured towards the battered old piano in the bay window, now covered with music manuscripts. 'Got a new one—I'm calling it *Variations on a Melting Snowflake*. Very Debussy, with boogie undertones.'

He tried to retreat beneath the covers again, but Jan's firm hand shook his shoulder. 'Get up anyway, darling, and come to the studio with me. What if Karas didn't give you a work-call? You can play him the new number and maybe he'll get them to buy the song for the next Bird Symphony; they need one.'

Guy rubbed his eyes and frowned. 'But dear, I don't want—'

'Sure, sure. You don't want to be in cartoons, you want New York publication and some day a recital and you'll have it. But we need money now, remember? And—and—' Jan's blue-violet eyes clouded a little. 'I thought you'd want to be around, for a day or so anyway.'

'Oh God, *that*!' He sat up stick-straight, looking shame-faced. 'I'd completely forgotten those nasty valentines and all the rest of it. Of course I'll come, and watch you like a hawk, too.'

'I was never watched by a hawk,' she said. 'By a wolf now and then, maybe, but never by a hawk.'

'Oh lord,' he muttered. 'To be clever so early in the morning.' He sighed. 'Okay. Hurry up with the bath, will you please?'

'You first,' said Janet magnanimously. 'I can dress in half the time it takes you, remember?'

'I remember.' He suddenly pulled her towards him, but Janet suddenly twisted away laughing.

'Too early in the morning, dear,' she said, and went hastily out of the room. Guy Fowler stared after her, sighing and muttering. There were times—and this was one of them . . .

'Women!' he said, and gingerly slid out of bed.

★

'Women!' said Mr Ralph Cushak somewhat later that morning, when he was advised by a pink-eyed Joyce that Miss Hildegarde Withers was outside and demanded to see him at once, with an A priority. 'Let her cool her flat heels for a minute,' he said. Then he looked at his secretary. 'Powder your nose or have a coffee or something. Didn't I tell you you could take the week off, by the way?'

'I'd rather be working,' the lush girl confessed, 'than sitting around home thinking about what happened to Larry. He was a heel, but a sorta sweet heel. And I always thought that some time—some time maybe—' She choked.

'Yes,' said Cushak, embarrassed.

'Mr Cushak?' Joyce came closer. 'It was an accident, wasn't it? That's what the police and the newspapers say. Is this Miss Withers trying to make something more of it?'

'She can't make anything more of it than it really was,' he pronounced. 'Your ex-husband died from the effects of poison-ivy, and nothing else. There's no question of—of—'

Joyce looked extremely relieved. 'Shall I show her in, then?' He nodded.

Miss Hildegarde Withers marched into the office with blood in her eye. Without any preliminaries she plunked down the statuette of Peter Penguin on his desk. 'And just what, Mr Cushak, do you know about *this*?'

He winced, and flushed a guilty flush. 'Plenty, as it happens.' Then he went on to explain. He had, some years ago when the big boss was on another business trip, ordered ten thousand of The Bird replicas from a persuasive ceramics salesman, as a sort of promotional give-away venture. After all, the idea had worked out with Donald Duck and Woody Woodpecker and why not here? Only it hadn't. The thing hadn't gone over and most of the figurines were still in boxes down in the basement. A few gross had been distributed throughout the studio or given to salesmen; by this time most of them had been taken home by studio employees for their children or else broken. There was no use trying to trace this particular one; anybody in the studio could have picked one up easily from somebody's desk or from the boxes in the basement. Cushak still didn't see why she was interested.

'I'm interested,' said the schoolteacher tartly, 'because it happens that this particular Bird came flying in my window early this morning, with a personal valentine attached.' She showed it to him.

Cushak's hands trembled just a little as he held the thing up to his bifocals and read aloud the doggerel verse. 'Good lord!' he said not irreverently. 'This grows more serious by the minute. Do you know, Miss Withers—I'm getting more and more convinced that this is no job for a lady, and I thought yesterday when you didn't show up that you must have somehow come to the same conclusion. Now I'm absolutely sure that if you continue at all you'll have to have competent assistance. Such as—'

'Such as some Mickey Spillane character? Perish forbid, young man. Besides, I have that assistance, in spades, doubled and redoubled.' Miss Withers had been hoping to bring the Inspector down to the studio this morning to get the lie of the land and meet the ostensible suspects, but Oscar Piper has chosen to high-tail it off into Los Angeles immediately after breakfast—without even offering to help her with the dishes. He was, she thought, probably punctili-ously reporting in at Spring Street as visiting policemen are traditionally supposed to do.

Anyway, there would be time for introductions later. Now she told Mr Cushak how she had spent yesterday. 'You see, young man,' she concluded, 'there *was* a Lucy, and *she* was run over by a car en route to one of your studio previews. You still insist that you never heard of her?'

Blankly he said, 'Of course I heard about the accident, but I never heard the poor woman's name and if I did I've forgotten it. The studio was not in any way involved, legally or morally—any more than you'd be if your maid was a passenger in a traffic accident.'

'Maid?' Miss Withers smiled. 'A little woman named

73

Hildegarde Withers comes in daily to do my housework. But I do see your point. I wish I saw the point of the murder —or perhaps it's *murders* now? Did everyone show up for work this morning, I hope?'

Cushak shrugged, and then went on to explain that most studio employees had a way of trickling in anywhere between nine and eleven. 'I've always thought,' he said, 'that we should have a time-clock for all artists to punch. But I suppose I could have Joyce check—'

'Never mind,' she interrupted hastily. 'It'll give me an excuse to snoop around a bit. Come, Talley.' Starting out, she whirled and came back to pick up the statuette of The Bird. 'I'll just keep this for evidence,' she said.

'But—but you can't find fingerprints on plaster,' Cushak told her.

She looked at him. 'Oh, so *you're* interested in criminology too? Then you must know that there are all sorts of evidence. Sometimes when in desperate straits I've had to manufacture it out of whole cloth.' She smiled, and went briskly out.

As schoolteacher and poodle came into the office which she now called her own, there was Tip Brown patiently waiting—and whiling away the time by studying the pencilled sketches, the doodles she had left on her desk day before yesterday. He looked up with a start. 'Oh, hello,' he said. 'You know, Miss Withers, some of these aren't bad at all. That frog swallowing a snake, and the tree with bottles of poison for fruit, and the skull and vines growing out of the eye-sockets . . .'

'Really?' she said, not unpleased.

'Yeah. Maybe you missed your calling. The stuff is a bit macabre for cartoons, though.'

'Miss Macabre, they call me. Or perhaps you never read Dickens?' She sat down. 'I'm surprised to see you today, Mr Brown. Surely you got drawings enough of my dog the other day to inspire a dozen movies?'

Tip Brown hesitated. 'It never does any harm to get plenty of action sketches.' Then he saw the cold look in her eye. 'Okay, ma'am. It wasn't *entirely* that. I just—I just

74

wondered if you had anything new on the murder?'

'The Reed death?' she countered cagily. 'But whatever would *I* know—'

'Don't kid me, lady. You're not here to work on The Circus Poodle—you don't give a damn about the story you're supposed to be assigned to. You've been asking sixteen thousand questions . . .' Tip looked faintly belligerent. 'Tell me, are you a private detective or something?'

'A private detective or nothing,' she said. 'But I didn't think it was so obvious; I must remember in future to wear dark glasses and a false beard.' She nailed him with her eye. 'By the way, since we're on the subject, I'd like to ask you a few more questions. Mr Brown, when the late Larry Reed played his perfectly hilarious practical joke on you and sent your mail out of town where it was lost for a month or so, just what important letters did you miss until too late?'

He sat down in a chair, rather hard. 'Oh, so you heard about that caper? I must have more un-friends around here than I thought. Well—it was—it was just that at the time I was somewhat married and my wife was in Reno getting the cure. She lost her money at the crap tables or got tight and sentimental in a bar or something—anyway she wrote me that she wanted to come back and start over. It was a letter I'd been sorta hoping for, because I was carrying a torch at the time. By the time I finally got the letter she'd changed her mind and figured I wasn't interested, and had up and married a singing cowboy who's master of ceremonies at a dude ranch. It was all settled, which was just as well, because believe me she was no bargain to live with and if she had come back it would just have been all to go over again. Larry didn't know it, but he accidentally did me a big favour with that corny gag.'

'Um—and did you realize your good fortune at the time?'

'Naturally not. I blew my top and said a lot of things— the same things somebody's repeated to you. But I cooled off . . .'

'Larry Reed got cooled off, too, to use the vulgar phrase. Forgive the personal questions, but somebody has to do something about it and I seem to be the one appointed. So—'

'So somebody has to do something about Jan!' he cut in. 'Isn't she actually in danger, real danger?'

Miss Withers shrugged. 'Perhaps, and perhaps not. It may be that the murderer is finished with his nefarious plans —or has been frightened off. It would appear that somebody wanted to kill Larry Reed, and built up this valentine thing and all the rest of it to cover the real motives.'

'Smoke-screen, huh? Or else a nut.' Tip nodded, and then frowned. 'But you must admit that Jan may be on the spot?'

'Certainly she may. And just why are you so much more worried about Miss Poole than the rest of your friends and associates who have been equally threatened?'

'There's only one Jan,' he said soberly.

She nodded. 'And of course there are two of Mr Karas and two of Mr Bayles?' As Tip Brown flushed pinker still, she added, 'And by the way, Mr Brown, can you tell me if all three of our potential victims are safe and sound in their offices this morning?'

Hesitantly Tip Brown admitted that while he knew nothing about the two men he had just happened to look in on Janet a little while ago and had found her working on the animation for *Peter Penguin's Sea-Serpent,* with a certain so-and-so piano player practically breathing down her fair white neck. 'That fellow!' he said. 'He's one that could stand watching; I've never liked musicians and never trusted 'em.'

'I have noticed that musicians are apt to be like other people. Does your antipathy to musicians extend to Mr Karas?'

Tip Brown snorted. 'That swell-headed maestro? Why, he actually thinks that the cartoons we make here are only backgrounds for his music instead of the other way around. Besides, the old goat is always making eyes at our sweater-girls—at his age!'

'Including Janet Poole?' The schoolteacher smiled. 'Relax, young man. I quite understand why you are interested in her, and I don't blame you. Love is a wonderful thing, they tell me—even unrequited love. But it is also often blind.'

He blinked. 'Well, I'm not blind enough to kid myself about my chances there; that piano-player with the phoney Boston accent has her hypnotized.'

'Perhaps not as completely as you think,' Miss Withers said wickedly. 'You know of course about Jan's posing—'

'What?' The round pink face paled. 'Who told you? Who'd dig that up now?'

'I mean about her posing for Larry Reed, at his home,' she probed quietly on.

'Oh,' he said in a different tone. 'I don't care who says it, it's not true. Sure, Jan went out with him a little when she first came to work here, but she'd never go up to that wolf-den of his alone—not even then.'

'But she did, and it must have been quite recently too,' continued the schoolteacher with elaborate casualness. 'Because there was a half-finished water-colour of her on his easel when he died.'

Tip Brown, who had been idly stroking Talleyrand's fuzzy top-knot, twisted the wool so hard that the poodle gave a reproachful 'Yipe' and scooted over to his corner. Tip carefully lighted a cigarette. 'So? Well, you never know, do you?' He waved his hand in a casual farewell gesture, and went hastily out.

'Well!' said Miss Withers to the dog. 'He either didn't know—or else he didn't know that anyone else knew. I'm talking about Jan's posing for the art class, of course. Her deep dark secret, like most secrets, was no secret at all. But he jumped at the idea of her posing for Larry Reed, even just for a portrait. That young man will bear watching—as who in this case won't? Among them a person named Rollo Bayles.'

Talley wagged his almost non-existent tail.

'No,' said Miss Withers firmly and shut him in the office, setting off briskly like a prospector looking for diamonds, or gold, but willing to settle for any sign of ore anywhere . . .

She found out that Bayles had a workroom in a long

building at the end of the studio street, and finally found a door with his name blazoned on it. She pushed inside without knocking, and found herself alone in a high narrow room smelling strongly of oil paints and lighted only from above; most of the wall space was given over to over-sized paintings in various stages of completion. They were all delicately, breathtakingly beautiful—if a bit on the vague side. The vagueness came, she realized, from the fact that in the compositions there was no central figures at all, no foci of interest; the paintings were all backgrounds against which some day the animated cartoon figures would perform their antics.

At the far end of the room a door bore a sign: 'Colour Lab.' A man's hat and raincoat hung on a hook near the door, though that was no proof that Rollo Bayles was on deck today—it might be only office camouflage, a permanent exhibit. Certainly the man was nowhere around; the place was silent as the proverbial tomb. She went immediately to the big paint-stained desk and without a qualm began to search it. Miss Withers long ago had come to the conclusion that a man's office desk—like a woman's handbag—is the key to his character.

Rollo Bayles, she thought, must be rather a messy type; he kept no order whatever and seemed to have spilled ink and paints rather freely about, even for an artist. There were no knick-knacks, no personal letters, but in one bottom drawer was a pile of ancient *Saturday Reviews*. For a moment the schoolteacher beamed, thinking that she and Mr Bayles had similar tastes—then she discovered that most of the magazines were open to the Personal columns, with a neat checkmark against such choice items as '*Is there a Costals for this lonely Solange, fond of outdoor sports and Existentialism? Write Box 233B.*'

'Dear me!' murmured Miss Withers, shaking her head. 'He's one of *those*.' But there were no evidences that Rollo Bayles had ever actually answered any of the lonely-heart ads. Probably, she thought, he had simply gloated over them, toyed with the idea of actually writing to one of those itching, waiting females; he had dreamed of wonderful new friendships and romances and at the same time had realized somewhere in the back of his mind that fairy princesses do not have to advertise for suitors.

As a last resort the schoolteacher looked under the blotter —men, she knew, always tucked things away under desk blotters—but there she found only a clipping from *Time* about a supposed new way to restore fading hair by means of a vitamin-complex pill, her own name and address and phone number on a scribbled bit of paper, and a print of the justly-famous calendar pin-up picture posed for by a certain young movie star. (According to *The Hollywood Reporter*, Miss Marilyn Monroe had said indignantly when asked by an interviewer if she'd had anything on when she posed, 'Of course! I had on some Chanel No. 5!')

But in spite of these sad lonely indications of 'the dreams of fair women' there was nothing at all to indicate any connection between Bayles and the late lamented Larry Reed—or any connection with the other recipients of the cross-eyed valentines. The thing just didn't fit together; Miss Withers felt somewhat like the audience at a magicians' show, sitting back and watching things that weren't where you thought they were.

'Misdirection,' she decided. And then her musings were interrupted by the sound of scuffling in the room behind the closed door, and she hastily withdrew from the vicinity of the desk and tried to look as if she weren't there. It was none too soon, for the door of the Colour Lab. burst open and a pretty auburn-haired lass of perhaps eighteen came loping through. She wore the blue uniform of a studio messenger, and she giggled as she ran. Close behind her but losing ground steadily was Rollo Bayles, already a bit winded.

The girl made the front door with a lead of five lengths, scooped up a pouch of still-undelivered mail, and slipped out into the sunshine with a last peal of merry laughter. Bayles stopped short, staring after her with an extremely odd expression on his face. He looked, Miss Withers thought, like a thwarted child—a tormented unhappy problem-child who might stamp his feet or smash something any minute. Then he turned and saw that he had an audience.

'*Mister* Bayles!' said Miss Withers drily. 'At this hour of the morning!'

The man regained control of himself quickly. 'I suppose you think—' he began. 'Well, it isn't like that at all. You see, I was only blending some colours to show her the exact shade of lipstick she should wear with that hair, and one thing led to another and—'

'And that isn't the point, young man. I'm not interested in your extra-curricular activities, if any. I just came here to return something of yours.'

'Mine?' Bayles stared blankly at the statuette of the sacred Bird. 'You're mistaken, ma'am.'

'The mistake was made by the person who hurled it through my window last night.'

Bayles stiffened warily. Searching his face, Miss Withers thought that she saw guilt there. But then people, as she knew, could feel guilt about so many different things. He blinked his rather protruding eyes, took a deep breath, and said, 'But why on earth—? Are you intimating that I'd do a thing like that? I'm supposed to be one of the targets of this crazy plot, remember?'

'This was the mistake that was made, Mr Bayles,' she went on coolly. 'While in the case of Larry Reed's murder there was no question of alibis—since we cannot know where and when and how he got the poison—now we *do* know that the murderer was in a car outside my bungalow at a certain time last night, leaving me a warning to lay off.'

'Oh?' he said cautiously.

'Yes.' She smiled brightly. 'You see what it means? This automatically eliminates everyone who has a good alibi for that hour. Immediately after the car roared away and before the driver had a chance to get home, I telephoned everyone involved in the case, just to check. You didn't answer your phone, by the way.'

'What? Oh, I can explain that. I'd taken a couple of

seconal tablets to knock myself out. The phone could have rung all night and I wouldn't have heard.'

'Then,' she persisted wickedly, 'you say you *were* home and in bed at three o'clock this morning?'

'Certainly. I came home shortly after two, and I can prove it. I always turn on my bedside radio for a little owl-music before I go to sleep, and the people in the next apartment heard it and pounded on the wall, so that proves—'

'That proves something, at any rate.' The schoolteacher felt a surge of secret triumph, though she also wished with all her heart that she *had* actually thought of making those phone-calls. She turned to go, and then as Bayles relaxed in obvious relief she whirled back on him again. 'Just one thing more,' she said. 'The sender of those poison-pen valentines knew too much about the past of his potential victims. Perhaps we can pursue that line a little. Mr Bayles, how did your secret leak out?'

The man shrugged helplessly. 'I don't know, honestly. It's nothing I'd be likely to talk about.'

'Not even to an old friend—or an affable bartender—or—?'

Bayles shook his head. 'For years I've put it out of my mind, completely. I wouldn't let myself think of it. You see, I promised my mother on her death-bed that I'd become a priest, and—and—' His eyes were wet and shining.

'I understand.' The schoolteacher took her departure, fearing that the man would break into *Mother Machree*—or into tears of self-pity. He was, she thought, a small loss to the Church of Rome. Miss Withers was beginning to form a picture of the real Rollo Bayles in her mind's eye, and it was as not as pretty as his paintings by any means.

Yet a man could be an apostate, he could break a death-bed promise to his adored mother, and still—could he be a murderer, could he kill, and kill with the subtle, sneaky method of poison?

The schoolteacher walked thoughtfully back along the sunlit studio street, past hurrying cutters with their precious cans of film, past cute little uniformed studio messengers with their languorous starlet's walk and their wondering starlit eyes—each remembering that Lana Turner had been a soda-jerk when she was discovered—past secretaries and electricians and executives and all the myriad denizens of this gold-plated ant-hill. From the open window of a sound room came the last line of the *alma mater* anthem—'G-g-g-gawk-wak—that's Peter Penguin's song . . .' repeated over and over again as the sound men ironed out indistinguishable errors in the track.

Miss Withers even ran into the gnomish janitor she had met on her first day here, who gave her a roguish wink. On an impulse she caught his sleeve. 'Mr Cassidy, you know more about this place than almost everyone. You knew Larry Reed, and all the others involved. Did he have any enemies? Who, do you think, would have a motive to poison him?'

'Poison?' The old man stiffened suspiciously. 'But the paper said—'

'The newspapers can be wrong, and so can the police.'

Mr Cassidy scratched his head. 'Well, if you ask me I'd say that Larry Reed was his own worst enemy. Coming into the studio with hangovers so bad that I had to go out and get him a pint so his hand would be steady enough to hold a pencil. Carrying a torch for some dame, he was.'

'His former wife?'

'Joyce—Mr Cushak's secretary? I don't think—'

'Janet Poole?'

'Maybe. I dunno. But ma'am, if Larry really was poisoned, I say they should look for a woman—because any fool knows that poison is *a woman's way*.'

Miss Withers thanked him and went on, more thoughtful still. Everyone nowadays seemed to be an amateur criminologist; everyone knew that poison is usually a feminine weapon, that writers of poison-pen letters always send one to themselves, and that the murderer *never* returns to the scene of his crime. All truisms. She remembered *Porgy and Bess*—'It ain't necessarily so.'

She came at last to the music stage and went up the steps, then through wide doors and into a good-sized hall, its walls draped with heavy cloth. Two bare overhead bulbs gave a dim glow—enough light so that she could see at one end a raised platform with a baby-grand piano, folding chairs and music-stands. The place was very empty and still, almost too still for her present mood. As the doors swung automatically shut behind her, they cut off all the cheerful noisy bustle of the studio, and the room was suddenly heavy with brooding silences; the dangling microphones and the hulking electrical equipment seemed to glare at her, reminding her that she was an intruder here.

Miss Withers almost expected the various complicated mechanisms to break into raucous music; she found herself holding her breath and tiptoeing as she went forward into the cool gloom. But all remained silent, too silent. She could see a smaller door at the far end of the place, and as she came closer she could make out that it bore the legend: 'Jules Karas, Music Director, Private.' She knocked once, and entered.

It was an office even larger than Mr Cushak's though somewhat less ornate. There was a Moviola, a big record-player, a bookcase stuffed with music sheets and orchestrations, and another case with stacks of phonograph records and albums. Under the one window was a desk; it was a very clean desk that bore only an onyx fountain-pen set, a plaster statuette of The Bird similar to the one she had in her hand, and an ashtray in which rested a half-smoked cigar in a long amber holder. Miss Withers felt somewhat relieved; at least all three of the people in whom she was most interested had shown up at the studio safe and sound this morning. The ash of the cigar in the tray was still warm to her exploring fingers, so she figured that she must have missed Mr Karas by seconds.

He might of course return at any moment. It was not the propitious time to go prowling in his desk as she had Mr Bayles's; on the other hand, there might never be another chance. She went to work swiftly and silently, and when she

83

had finished with the last neat drawer she knew nothing about Mr Karas that she had not known before—except that he kept a large, oddly-shaped bottle of something labelled *slivowitz* in his desk, tucked in behind rolls of music manuscript. The stuff smelled somewhat of old prunes and heavily of alcohol, and it made her sneeze.

From the doorway behind her, a pleasant masculine voice said, 'If you're needing a snort, go ahead. Don't mind me.'

The schoolteacher whirled around, almost dropping the brandy bottle, to see Guy Fowler standing there, a sheet of music manuscript in his hand and an expression of amused surprise on his face. She hastily replaced the bottle and slammed the drawer. 'I was looking for Mr Karas,' she said.

'Well,' pointed out the young man reasonably, 'you're not likely to find him in his desk drawer.' He came on into the room. 'Matter of fact, I'm looking for him too; I've got a new song-number Jan wants me to try on him. But I guess he must have popped out for a cup of coffee or something.'

'He's obviously not here, at any rate,' Miss Withers snapped. 'What's wrong?'

Guy Fowler was staring at the ashtray on Karas's desk, with a very odd expression. 'I don't know. But I never knew Karas to go anywhere without that holder; when he wasn't smoking he kept it in his breast pocket. He surely must have left here in a tearing hurry. And he *never* hurries.'

'"The Ides of March are here, la grippe is at the door—and many folks are dying now, who never died before."' The schoolteacher sniffed. 'So you think Mr Karas left here in a hurry. Frightened, perhaps? Do you suppose he got another of those valentines?'

'Could be,' the young man said. 'They seem to be falling like autumn leaves, don't they?' His look was wise and knowing and most sympathetic.

'So you know that I too received one, in the middle of the night?'

His smile was faintly amused. 'Of course. You don't know this studio very well, Miss Withers. It's one big happy family, with no secrets—especially at a time like this, with the whole lot buzzing. Secretaries overhear things and then drop a word to some pal around the water-cooler or in the coffee-shop—that's the way it goes.'

'The most important secret of all seems still to be pretty well kept,' she told him. 'Don't forget that the murderer of Larry Reed is among us, laughing up his sleeve.'

'His?' Guy Fowler echoed softly.

'Of course. The only girl who seems to be involved in this is Janet, and certainly you're not suggesting—'

He almost laughed out loud. 'Certainly I wasn't. Janet wouldn't kill anybody, and if she did—by some fantastic trick of fate—she couldn't keep the secret for ten minutes. She's as clear as a mountain brook . . .'

'Hmmm,' murmured Miss Withers. There were things young Mr Fowler would be learning when he married his clear mountain brook, or she missed her guess.

'I was only thinking,' he continued thoughtfully, 'that in all the books and stuff I've read on the subject poison is supposed to be a woman's weapon, no?'

Here we went again. Miss Withers sighed and nodded. She could have mentioned such notable exceptions as Molineux and Carlyle Harris and Dr Palmer and the unfortunate Crippen, but Guy Fowler still was talking. 'What about Joyce Reed—Mr Cushak's bumptious secretary who used to be married to Larry?'

The schoolteacher looked at him. 'Any special reason for bringing her name into the case?'

'No, ma'am. But when people are married, or have been—'

'They're automatically suspect if anything happens to one of them. I know—and it's a sad commentary on the marriage state. But frankly, Joyce doesn't look like a poisoner to me.'

'If it really was poison.'

'It really was, and not the first time this particular poison was used, either.'

Guy's ears perked up. *'What?'*

But Miss Withers had already, as usual, said more than she intended. 'Excuse me, young man—'

She started out, but he blocked her way, looking suddenly very boyish and engaging. 'Why don't you like me, Miss Withers?'

'I beg pardon?' She drew back, staring at him. 'I think I'll answer that question with another. Why are you such a fool as to refuse to marry your Janet until you've paid back every last cent you've borrowed from her? That may take a long time and she doesn't want money, she wants you. Now.'

His face set. 'A man has his pride.'

'Which always goeth before a fall, or so I've heard.'

'You don't understand. I've been dodging responsibilities most of my life, and I guess running away from things. I'm going to be standing on my own two feet from now on.'

'*Men!*' said Miss Hildegarde Withers in her most spinsterly voice, and pushed past him and out of the place. But when she looked back over her shoulder, she saw young Fowler still standing there, scratching his head and looking puzzled. But it was nothing to the puzzlement that possessed her as she hurried back to her office. There she cut Talleyrand's welcome home scene as short as possible, shaking hands only once instead of the usual baker's dozen, and sat herself down with pencil and note-book. 'Rollo Bayles . . .' she wrote, and had filled hardly half a page when the telephone shrilled at her elbow like an offended bumblebee. 'Yes, Mr Cushak?' she answered wearily.

But it wasn't Mr Cushak at all; it was the Inspector, and his voice was jubilant. 'Hildegarde? Remember I told you that I'd solve this case for you today?'

CHAPTER 7

'Second thoughts, they say, are best.'

—DRYDEN

The Inspector had—as Miss Withers guessed—paid his courtesy call at Spring Street first thing that morning, tactfully concealing of course his surprised amusement that the third largest and fastest-growing city in America should still be operating with police machinery which even Yonkers would have considered archaic.

The chief of detectives with whom he exchanged courtesies and a cigar had very little to say about the Larry Reed case, though Piper tried to pump him gently. Poison-ivy was poison-ivy, and some people were more allergic to it than others, and the whole thing had been dropped.

'Yeah,' said the Inspector.

The other man stared at him through a blue haze of cigar smoke. 'You out in our fair city on official business, Inspector?'

'I haven't had a vacation in years,' said Piper truthfully if not exactly frankly. They ended at that, with a polite handshake.

And the Inspector was off for Forest Lawn. It was not, he found, as simple as it sounded. There were several Forest Lawns scattered here and there about the city of Los Angeles —and the city of Los Angeles had a strange way of becoming something else again within the confines of its own boundaries; it was Beverly Hills or Burbank or Glendale when you least expected it. But finally by the process of elimination he ran down the right Forest Lawn, a vast green place of rolling hills and trees and flowers like no other cemetery he had ever seen. It should be, he thought, more of a tourist attraction than the beaches or the Hollywood Bowl or the La Brea pits; it was sunny and pleasant and ornamented with expensive marble statuary and churches and chapels and auditoriums, but with no melancholy tombstones. It also had a very businesslike office, which he found after some difficulty. A professionally grave and sympathetic young man in a blue suit and bow tie instead of the usual funereal afternoon clothes of the undertaker's assistant greeted him at the door. There was a slight misunderstanding of a few seconds while the Inspector explained that he did not at the moment require any professional services.

'It's about Lucy—Lucinda Wersbeck,' he said. 'You

planted—I mean you buried her something more than a year ago.'

The young man nodded. 'Wersbeck, Lucinda,' he said to one of the three secretaries behind the desk. 'Locate it, please.'

'But I don't—'

'It's no trouble at all. In a place this size we have to have an efficient mapping system, or we wouldn't be able to function. It'll only be a minute.'

'BC-16,' spoke up the girl, who had been at the filing case.

The young man moved over to a wall map. 'With those coordinates,' he said, 'we can locate any place of interment in a few seconds. You see? Here it is. I'm afraid it's well across the park—do you have a car? If not, possibly we can arrange to have someone drive you up there.' He was pointing to a rather distant point on the map.

'I don't have a car,' said the Inspector rather testily. 'And there is nothing in the world I would rather not do than visit Lucinda Wersbeck's grave, or any grave. I am a police officer—' he showed his gold badge in its leather case—'and I only want to ask some questions.'

The young man stiffened a little. 'A Los Angeles or Glendale officer?'

'New York. And—'

'If there is any question of disinterment I'm afraid we'll have to ask for a court order or at least a request from the surviving next of kin—'

'I don't want to dig her up, God forbid I should disturb her poor bones. I only want certain information; I want to know who paid for the undertaking fees and the burial plot.'

'Well!' said the young man. 'May I ask why?'

'You may, and I'll tell you. The Wersbeck woman was a pauper; she was struck by an automobile and later died in the County Hospital. But she wound up in these plush surroundings—somebody paid for that, and it fits into a homicide investigation I'm working on. I want to find out who.'

88

The young man looked pained. 'I'm sorry, Inspector, but you seem to have fallen in with an unfortunately widespread delusion. Our rates here are not higher than other burial parks, and sometimes lower; we adapt to the purse of the bereaved. Our funeral services, including the last services for the dead—'

'Yes, yes,' cried Oscar Piper. 'But it must have cost something, and somebody paid the tab. Somewhere in your records you must have that information, and I want it.'

'I'm afraid I cannot give out that information—'

The Inspector crossed to a phone that stood on the counter. He dialled, and waited a moment. 'Is this Michigan 5211? I want to speak to Chief Parker please . . .'

He felt his sleeve plucked at. 'There's no need for that, Inspector. It you'll wait just a moment, I'm sure that we can get the information you need.'

Piper hung up. 'Well, get it,' he said.

The secretary went back to the filing case, and finally came forth with the information that the undertaking and burial expenses for Miss Lucinda Wersbeck had been paid for by someone who'd signed 'Mr P. R. F.'

'Initials yet!' said the Inspector. 'Funny business here, if I ever saw it. Was it by cash or cheque or what?'

The records didn't show, but the bill of $350 had been paid, in advance of burial. That was all they knew.

'Can I speak to the clerk who made the transaction?'

There was some more delay while an examination was made of the initials on the ledger. 'I'm afraid you cannot.'

'And why not?'

'Because Miss Lotta Earle left our employ about that time. I'm sorry.'

'You'll be sorrier if you don't dig up her last known home address.'

It was hastily dug up, and the Inspector departed with it scribbled on a sheet of memo paper, still not entirely discouraged. The person, presumably a man, who had paid for Lucinda Wersbeck's funeral expenses had concealed himself behind initials. 'Mr P. R. F.'—Oscar Piper wanted a description of that individual, and soon. Because he felt himself to be on one of the hottest trails in his history.

He found Miss Lotta Earle—quite obviously Mrs Lotta Earle—in a little house in Burbank, nursing a beer and a fat new baby, with an older boy in sagging underdrawers hanging to her skirts or where her skirts would have been if she had worn any. She was, perhaps because of the beer and the warm influence of the sunlight on the large portions of her body showing above and beneath her shorts, quite cooperative, and offered the Inspector a seat on the lawn and a can of beer, the first of which he accepted.

'Sure I remember the guy,' said Lotta. 'It was about the last deal I handled before I left the Lawn. He wanted everything handled nice, but as cheap as possible . . .'

'Describe him,' Piper said.

She shut her eyes. 'After so long a time—but I'll try. He was about medium size, nicely-dressed. Not young, not old.'

'That is quite a description, young lady. It could apply to almost anybody.'

She frowned in concentration. 'Well—he was smoking a cigar, and he had an accent.'

'What sort of accent? Spanish, German, or a good Irish brogue like me own grandad's?'

The lady wasn't sure. 'It was just an accent,' she said. 'That's all I seem to remember.'

'And maybe that's enough,' said Oscar Piper, rising from the grass. 'Where's the nearest pay-phone?'

It turned out to be twelve blocks down the street, and he was out of breath when he reached it. Then he had further difficulties with the phone, being under the mistaken impression that a nickel was still legal currency. But finally he got through to the studio and to Hildegarde Withers.

'So as I've said, I've solved it,' he insisted.

'Not really!' Her voice sounded flat.

'I saw right off when you told me the setup last night that you'd missed the essential point about Lucy. Lucinda Wersbeck died in a county hospital as a charity patient and was taken to the Morgue, yet she was buried at Forest

90

Lawn. The tab was paid by a Mr P. R. F.—know anybody with those initials, or anybody who would use them?'

Miss Withers thought. 'Not offhand, Oscar.'

'Well, somebody paid, and I'm on his trail.'

'Well, Oscar? I'm all ears.'

"All nose, you mean. Anyway, it was so long ago that nobody remembers too much about it, but I have a description of the man.' He told her.

'Good gracious!' she gasped. 'But—but that description fits Mr Karas, the music director here at the studio. Only he was in the car that killed Lucinda Wersbeck, and he was the recipient of one of the murder valentines!'

'Okay,' the Inspector said with some natural complacency. 'So it fits. Everybody knows and you should know too that the sender of poison-pen letters always sends one to himself. You better keep a close eye on the guy until I can get over there. How do I get to the studio from a phone-booth in a drugstore on a side street in Burbank, huh?'

'Why—just a minute, Oscar. I can't hear you; somebody's shouting . . .' Her voice trailed away and was lost. Yet she hadn't hung up and they hadn't been cut off, because he could hear a faint tantalizing rumble of voices at the other end of the line.

'Hello? Hello-ello-ello?'

He waited there sweating in the tight little phone booth for the better part of a cigar, now and then at the request of the operator fishing another dime out of his pants pocket and losing it for ever in the maw of the insatiable machine. At long last he heard a familiar voice at the other end. 'Oscar?'

'Yes,' he snapped back bitterly, 'this is Oscar, the Forgotten Man, some dollar or so poorer than he was half an hour ago. What may I ask—?'

'You were asking me how to get from Burbank to the studio,' she said, in an odd tone. 'Take a street car or a bus or walk; don't bother with a taxi because there's no hurry about your putting the handcuffs on Mr Karas. He's not

91

even here; they just took him away in an ambulance, I believe dying or dead—'

'What in the name of holy St Paul and Minneapolis—?' he gasped. 'Not—not again?'

'Yes, again. Same method.'

'You sure?'

'Yes, it appears to be another use of poison-ivy—more of "the weed of hell".' she sniffed. 'At least they say he showed all the symptoms. It does seem to be catching, doesn't it?'

'But—but he fitted the description so well!'

'I'm very much afraid, Oscar, that Mr Karas fits nothing at the moment except a short, over-width coffin.'

'But Lucy—'

'"Lucy is dead and in her grave—" and you might as well stay there and keep vigil over it for all the help you're being in this case. Solve it for me today, didn't you say? Excuse me, Oscar, I am wanted by a big man with a badge who is lurking in my doorway. Goodbye.' And she hung up, very firmly.

CHAPTER 8

'Some men's whole delight is . . . to talk of a cock and bull over a pot.'

—Burton

That, as they say, tore the lid off.

A few minutes after Guy Fowler came rushing out of the music stage to announce that he had found Mr Karas strangling to death in the men's washroom, the big studio resembled nothing so much as an ant-hill stirred by a stick. At first, because of his wild look and dishevelled hair, there were those who imagined that the part-time musician had been at Karas's well-known bottle of *slivowitz* and was making it all up, but he managed to convince somebody who went to see—and then screamed for the ambulance.

Throughout the entire place, pens and pencils and brushes were tossed aside, screens went dark in the projection room; reels stopped reeling film through the sprockets of editorial and the cutters' scissors were still. The merry madcap laughter of Peter Penguin was some minutes later drowned out by the wolf-wail of police sirens. A black battered sedan swung in on screeching tyres through the main auto-gate of the studio and—with no hesitation at all—roared through the sacrosanct streets until it came to Cartoon Alley.

From it erupted a burly police detective in what Miss Hildegarde Withers would have called 'plain-clothes'—he himself called it 'citizen-dress' after the prevailing fashion in official circles—though there was certainly nothing plain about him, he wore lavender slacks and a Hawaiian shirt covered with hibiscus flowers, plus a cowboy belt.

But lavender slacks or no, in ten minutes he had set up a temporary inquisition in Karas's office, backed by three blue-blacked uniformed officers who had immediately set about herding into the main music stage everyone who could possibly know anything about the case and a great many who couldn't. They milled there, like alarmed sheep. Finally herded into the edge of their musicians' folding chairs, they eyed one another with a new dubiousness. There was strain in the air; there was also a faint note of embarrassment, for each one of them knew that in Hollywood's four decades and more there had never been a proved case of murder or attempted murder inside a studio. And it had had to happen *here*.

Sergeant Callan, a massive thumb-fingered man in the Hawaiian shirt, whose brick-red face attested that he had spent most of his career writing traffic tickets in the bright summer sunlight of the Valley, appeared suddenly in the inner office doorway when they were all gathered together, and essayed a brief speech which was not obviously his forte. 'Just keep your pants on, folks—' he began, and then remembered where he was.

He remembered that the studios, and this studio in particular, paid more into the local till in taxes than did almost any industry. He remembered that half the people he knew worked in a studio or were married to or divorced from or at least friends with somebody who depended on the motion picture industry and its ramifications for their livelihood. It might be best to go a bit slowly, Sergeant Callan thought —at least until he was a little surer of his ground.

'I mean, ladies and gents,' he continued, 'that if you'll be a bit more quiet and cooperative, we'll get this over with fast and you can all go to lunch.' The sergeant tried—not too successfully—to be one of the boys. 'Okay?'

Nobody said anything, though Sergeant Callan seemed to be waiting for applause, like the acrobats first on the vaudeville bill who come out and bow and wait and hope.

From where Miss Hildegarde Withers sat on the sidelines, nobody in the crowd seemed to be thinking about lunch, though it was well after twelve. She was watching them like the proverbial hawk, hoping for a clue; clues were scarce today. Her favourite suspects—and all the other suspects too—were trying to be self-possessed.

She could see Rollo Bayles sitting in the back row, chewing surreptitiously on his cuticle, having already evidently finished his nails. Joyce Reed, the flamboyant secretary who had once been married to the first victim of this particular murder cycle, was either crying into her handkerchief or hiding behind it—it was beyond the schoolteacher at the moment to tell which, but she made certain inner commitments to find out a little more about Joyce. Probably because —as everybody kept telling her—'poison is a *woman's* way'.

'Truisms,' said the schoolteacher to herself. 'And you can have them, for all of me.' Murders, she had observed, were not always committed or solved according to the rules. They were usually solved by observation and deduction, by perseverance and a little blind luck. She could use some of that luck now.

She looked at Mr Cushak, standing at the very opposite side of the room from his lush secretary; it was evidently beneath his dignity to sit down beside the employees. The man stood with his hands clasped behind his back and his lips pressed more tightly than ever together. Now and then he looked at his watch, possibly wondering about appointments missed and about the inevitably-bad newspaper publicity the whole thing would entail. Perhaps he was wondering what he would say to the big boss in New York when he had to call him on long-distance and break the news. Cushak, for whatever reason, was not a happy man.

Miss Withers studied him carefully, and admitted to herself that he stood low on the list of suspects. Even though there were sometimes hidden turmoils deep inside these prim, conventional men, not even her active imagination could picture him as a murderer; certainly not as a murderer who smoke-screened his act with this theatrical nonsense about death-warnings in the shape of left-handed valentines. Though of course the combination of a rich successful executive with a Cadillac and a flamboyantly beautiful divorcée secretary to whose charms he was exposed every day might just possibly—She shook her head. Even if they were carrying on, why should either or both try to get rid of Larry Reed, the husband she had got rid of legally a long time ago —to say nothing of Mr Karas? The truth must lie deeper down than that.

Continuing her keen-eyed scanning of the principal figures in the case, she came to Tip Brown sitting with several other artist-writers in the middle row of chairs just behind a group of giggling little messenger-girls. The others were engaged in whispered badinage with the young ladies, which was only natural under the circumstances. Tip's pink round face was calm, but in his lips was a sodden, sagging cigarette that he had somehow forgotten to light. He was watching Janet Poole up front, a strange new frightened Jan. Miss Withers saw the girl turn and catch his eye and manage a smile that was a travesty of a smile, done with her soft wide lips and with no eyes involved in it at all. Jan's shoulders were slumped and her bright blonde hair somehow had lost its sheen, as a tropical fish out of water loses its rainbow colours. At this moment Jan looked all of her 28 years and more; the veneer was off and she looked something of the Polska peasant again. Guy Fowler, sitting beside her, their shoulders touching, seemed somewhat calm and disinterested; perhaps somewhat pleased with himself, like a famous dramatic critic watching a poor play and planning what devastating things he was going to write about it . . .

And in the far corner sat Cassidy, in his work-coveralls, smoking a blackened pipe and obviously enjoying the drama of it all. It was evident to Miss Withers that Cassidy's attitude towards the studio people of this era was that of Talleyrand towards cats; anything that happened to them was much too good for them. The man was thinking, perhaps, of the great days he had known here within these walls and stages, the days of Laura La Plante and Norman Kerry and Vilma Banky—all gone for ever.

From her seat on the sidelines, the schoolteacher watched and waited; watched the stirred ant-hill in which somewhere there was a scorpion. Well, to continue the analogy, she herself could perhaps be a spider—or could a spider spin a web in which to entangle a scorpion? Lost in a maze of questions to which she could put no immediate answer, she suddenly heard Sergeant Callan turn again to the assemblage—he had perhaps been keeping them waiting for psychological reasons—and say, 'Okay. So first off, I want a statement from the one that found the body—I mean the victim.'

Janet Poole suddenly let go of Guy's hand, automatically straightened his tie, and patted him encouragingly on the shoulder. He set his jaw and started to rise, then hesitated as he saw a wiry, grizzled little man, dressed in the conservative blue suit and black shoes of Manhattan, push his way briskly to the front and buttonhole the sergeant in charge. The officer scowled and started to give the newcomer a brush-off, and then caught a glimpse of the gold badge cupped in Inspector Oscar Piper's right hand. There was a change in the atmosphere and then a quick exchange of whispers. Callan nodded and stepped aside, beckoning. The Inspector started inside, but at that point there came the quick patter of feet. Miss Withers appeared, as usual, out of nowhere.

'Wait, Oscar! Wait for me!' she cried.

Sergeant Callan turned back and looked at her doubtfully. Then he turned back to Piper. 'This lady with you, Inspector?'

Oscar Piper, perhaps remembering certain remarks made over the telephone not too long ago, said quietly, 'Not at the moment,' and went on inside, leaving the schoolteacher speechless with indignation. The door of the inner office closed firmly behind them, and as she reached for the knob a large uniformed policeman took her firmly by the arm and suggested that maybe she better go back and *siddown*.

He stood before the door, arms akimbo, and so she gave him a withering Withers look and went back and sat down, fuming quietly. '*Men!*' she said, almost out loud.

Miss Withers was not one to wait quietly, ever. For a little while she tried to amuse herself and pass the time by playing eenie-meenie-miney-mo among the potential suspects, coming out usually by the same door through which she went in. Almost everyone in the room looked guilty, in varying degrees. But that was a way people had, even spotlessly innocent people, in circumstances like this. Perhaps the most innocent looking would be the one; she worked at that idea for a while, coming out at last to the conclusion that it was a toss-up between Tip Brown and Joyce Reed, with perhaps a shade to the former. Neither of them had even received one of the valentines. The schoolteacher began to get bored with sitting, after a while. There was only one policeman in the room; she waited until his back was turned and then drifted casually towards the exit, slipping out without the ghost of a sound. Something had to be done, and soon. From what she had seen of Sergeant Callan, and from what she knew about the Inspector, bless him, it wasn't going to be done here and now. The roots of this thing ran deep down. She went quickly back to her office and across the deserted studio street, and got on the telephone.

Meanwhile, inside what had once been Mr Karas's office, the professional formalities were over. Sergeant Callan was obviously enjoying one of the Inspector's clear-Havana *puros*, amid a cloud of blue smoke. 'We don't mind having a homicide expert from New York in this thing with us,' he was conceding. 'Not that the case is actually homicide yet —this Karas guy hasn't quite turned up his toes. I just called the hospital and they say he's got a chance, though he's still on the critical list. But I also got in touch with Spring Street, and they say there at downtown homicide that because of this they're going to re-open the Larry Reed case; the house where he died is in their jurisdiction and not ours, you know.'

'I didn't know, exactly,' Oscar Piper admitted. 'Los Angeles and its boundaries and jurisdictions are a bit too much for a New Yorker—not to speak of some of its people.'

Callan scratched his head. 'I guess I see what you mean, all right. You have to live out here—'

'God forbid!' said the Inspector.

'Okay. But seriously, I don't get this stuff about poison-ivy. I thought it was only supposed to be a nasty weed that makes people turn red if they handle it carelessly—you get an itch and little blisters, and you use brown soap and usually it goes away.' The sergeant paused. 'No?'

'No, not entirely,' Piper said. 'Quite right, however, in most cases. But we're dealing with what seems to be an insidious concentrate of the stuff; it's to poison-ivy what TNT is to a firecracker. And I think personally that it's been used for two murders, and three if this Karas guy dies. Let me give you a last fill-in, Sergeant. Four years ago last December 24th a Manhattan night-club dancer named Zelda Bard received a gift-wrapped bottle of rare old Napoleon brandy through the mails. Of course we all know that all brandy bottled since 1900 is labelled Napoleon brandy, but she took it as a rare compliment. Zelda was a tall, exotic doll who got around considerably; I have a list here of her boyfriends and it's as long as your arm. She probably had a lot of others who aren't on the list, as she didn't keep books. From what we gathered at Centre Street she was mostly a teaser—none of them came home with her, though she accepted diamond and emerald bracelets when indicated, without a qualm. Anyway—the gift card had some-how been left out of the package, and her maid had stupidly put the wrappings down the incinerator before our men got there, so we hadn't much to go by. But after the lovely Zelda got home from her last performance that night, she made herself a couple of quick highballs from the gift bottle—and she was found dead in her bed next morning. I'll show you the report of our medical examiner, Dr Bloom, who found that she had been strangled to death, but not with human hands. The mucous membranes of her nose and throat were terribly engorged, there was considerable lividity of the face, and her limbs were contorted. The final verdict of our medical examiner was acute allergic reaction, caused by a heavy overdose of—' (here the Inspector consulted his notebook)—'of *toxicondendron radicans*, or—in other words, of poison-ivy.'

Sergeant Callan rubbed his heavy chin with a thick red thumb. 'That's a new one.'

'Not just new to you, it was new to us at Centre Street too. Dr Bloom got personally interested in the case, though he usually leaves these things to his assistants. He did a lot of research on it, and you're most welcome to what we have.' Oscar Piper brought out his voluminous brief-case. 'According to Bloom, and the best available authorities, poison-ivy and its close cousin poison-oak aren't poisons at all, they're allergens.'

'I'm allergic only to my wife's mother,' Callan said with heavy humour. 'I break out when she comes around—usually I just break out of the house and go down to a bar. But, Inspector, I had a dose of poison-ivy once. I broke out practically all over.' He shook his head. 'It ain't fatal.'

'As we have said, it's "the weed of hell". It hits different people in different ways. You can handle it with impunity for years—that's a good word, impunity—and then you suddenly get hit by it. There is no true immunity to it except in Eskimos and in infants up to the age of about a year, don't ask me why. According to Dr Bloom, who took the time to do considerable research in the thing, the basic

99

element of poison-ivy is something absolutely inimical to the human system, almost as if the weed had been transplanted here from Mars or some place.' Piper shrugged. 'Some authorities think that there's an essential, non-volatile oil in the plant; others hold that the reaction is caused by a malignant spore like ergot, only ergot is a fungus parasite infecting grain and not a real plant at all. Anyway, to get down to cases, we found out that some years ago in the graduate school at Marksville University they put on an experimental project as part of advanced research in the field of allergies, and they happened to find a way of concentrating poison-ivy into an almost tasteless, colourless oil. They made a couple of quarts of the concentrate, using a new process; one drop of the stuff on a man's arm would make him break out like a bad boil. After the experiments were over they published their results and methods in an obscure pamphlet that nobody ever read, and forgot the whole thing. But it wouldn't have been impossible for some chemistry student to have had access to the deadly stuff while it was still around the lab.; it would have been fairly easy for anyone with a smattering of chemistry and botany to have repeated the processes by which they concocted it . . .'

'Wait a minute,' interrupted Sergeant Callan. 'In those experiments, did anyone try tasting it?'

'Luckily for them, no. But our medical examiner says that the mucous membranes of the body are the most sensitive parts—sensitive to allergens, I mean. Some doctors believe that coryza, the common cold, is only an allergy. Anyway, a few months after the Marksville thing was published, Zelda Bard, an exotic night-club dancer, died horribly from poison-ivy laced with brandy.'

The sergeant shook his head stubbornly. 'But folks don't *die* from allergies!'

'Not usually, but Dr Bloom says it has happened. He told me about a case ten years or so ago out on Long Island. A girl out at Oyster Bay who was very allergic to tuna-fish went out for a Sunday sail with some friends on Long Island

100

Sound. The cook who put up the picnic lunches ran out of chicken and sneaked some tuna into the sandwich spread. The girl unknowingly ate three sandwiches and a few minutes later came down with an attack. The wind died down·and the sloop was becalmed or stuck or whatever they call it. Anyway, by the time they got back to shore the girl was dead as Kelsey.'

Sergeant Callan unhappily studied the ash of his cigar, obviously wishing he was back on his motor cycle again. 'So, Inspector, you're saying that you think there's maybe a link between your Zelda Bard case and the death of Larry Reed and now this Karas thing I'm stuck with?'

'I very much suspect it. Only times this particular poison has been used, to my knowledge—and we get pretty accurate reports from all over the country, and from abroad.'

Callan nodded. 'That list of your dead dancer's boyfriends —was the name of any of these studio people there?'

'No. But people have been known to change their names, and it's likely that we didn't list half of the men she knew —or the men who would have liked to know her. From her photographs she was a *dish*.' The Inspector gave out with a man-to-man wink. 'There's no pinning it down by age-groups either; the Bard girl seems to have played the field, anything in pants from sixteen to sixty, and left them all— as far as we could find out—gasping and feeling foolish.' The Inspector shook his head. 'I don't know, Sergeant, but maybe it's about time for you to huddle with my friend Miss Hildegarde Withers, the hatchet-faced old biddy who tried to crash the gate a few minutes ago.' He explained briefly why the ex-schoolteacher was in the studio, and about the poison-pen valentines.

'Oh, come now, Inspector!' Callan waved his cigar. 'It sounds—'

'Okay, I confess that I thought at the beginning that this was a false alarm, which was why I turned Hildegarde loose on it, thinking that she was just the one to cope with poison-pen valentines. Only it turned out to be serious, which is why I flew out.'

'We got a nut,' decided Sergeant Callan. 'And they say it takes one to catch one.' He turned towards the uniformed man at the door. 'Get this Withers dame in here pronto.'

It was easier said than done. But the schoolteacher was finally located in her office, still on the telephone. Officially escorted back to the music stage and planted on a chair in the inquisitorial office, she had her say. She also displayed the only two trick valentines available—Larry Reed's and her own. She brought them up to date on all that had transpired, with only a few minor reservations. Sergeant Callan, perspiringly, made notes as she talked.

'Penguins and stuff,' he said. 'It's an inside job, obviously. Now maybe we're getting somewhere! Huh!' His huh was hopeful. 'This Lucy thing—'

'Now maybe we're getting *nowhere*,' the schoolteacher interrupted. 'We're going down seventeen blind-alleys all at once. I happen to know a hawk from a handsaw, and also a red herring when I see it dragged right out in front of my eyes.'

'But the description of the man who paid her funeral expenses fits Mr Karas and nobody else?' Callan licked his pencil and made some more notes.

'Maybe it does,' grudgingly admitted the schoolteacher. 'And the use of initials is suspicious. But it still makes no sense to me. Karas was one of the passengers in the car that struck Lucy, he was one of the recipients of the left-handed valentines, and now he's in the hospital supposed to be dead or dying. Are you gentlemen trying to suggest that he should also be an old swain of hers, setting out at this late date to avenge her and then somehow getting a dose of his own medicine—no, *no*! I can swallow some coincidences, but not that.'

'He could have taken a tiny dose of the poison as a blind,' suggested the Inspector. 'And it could have hit him harder than he planned; we know that sensitivity to the weed varies with the individual.'

'Fiddlesticks,' said Miss Withers.

'But where else to look?' put in Sergeant Callan.

'How about looking for one of the employees of this studio who was in New York City four years ago this Christmas, and sent Zelda Bard the brandy?' The Inspector sat back and waited.

Miss Withers sniffed, but Callan was already giving orders to have the studio people brought in for questioning, one at a time. As his visitors made no move to go, the sergeant shrugged and said, 'I guess you can both stick around if you want to, since you're in it this far.'

'I had no intention of leaving, unless forcibly ejected,' Miss Withers told him. 'After all, this is *my* case.'

Guy Fowler was first on the list, a young man somewhat worried beneath his surface sophistication and faintly on the defensive, though trying hard to appear otherwise. His statement—taken down in shorthand by a bored policeman —was short and to the point; he had come down to the studio today—even though he had not had a work-call— because he had hoped to get Mr Karas to listen to a new number that he had just composed last night. The music manuscript was produced in evidence. Guy said he had noticed that Karas had left his treasured cigar-holder and most of a perfectly good cigar on the desk, which was very unlike him. That had started the young man wondering—'

'I can attest to that part of it,' Miss Withers put in. 'I was here.'

'Thanks,' he said. 'So as I said, I started wondering what would take him off in such a hurry; I thought maybe he'd got another of the valentine notes or something. I waited around a bit and he didn't come back, so I started looking for him. The first place I looked was the—the washroom, and there he was, doubled up on the floor like—'

'Like a pretzel?' the schoolteacher suggested helpfully.

Sergeant Callan glared at her, the Inspector concealed a grin, and Guy nodded. 'I suppose you could put it like that. His face was all red and swollen—'

'Like a poisoned pup?' Miss Withers prompted.

'You might say so, yes.'

'You might also say that those that hide can find, too,'

103

said Callan with professional nastiness. 'Maybe you knew that something had happened to the guy, and maybe you *knew* where to look.'

The young man stiffened.

'Can you deny that you were in New York City four years ago last Christmas?' This last from the Inspector.

'I can indeed,' Guy Fowler said. 'If it matters, and I don't see why, I was up in New Haven at Eli Yale's University, not having the money for a week-end in New York or Boston and not wanting to go home for the holidays and have my father harp on my grades all the time. That I can prove— I was practically the only man in my dormitory that week.' He stood up. 'Am I being accused of having tried to murder Mr Karas, and if so, how and why?'

'Siddown, young man. The *how* is easy. It was done with a concentrate of poison-ivy administered in some way—' Callan scratched his head.

'If you ask me, which nobody has, it was probably planted in a bottle of some foul brew called *slivowitz* which I just happened to see in that desk over there this morning,' Miss Withers pointed out. 'Just as Larry Reed was killed with the same nasty stuff put into the bottle of mineral oil he kept in his office, and which later disappeared. I suppose the *slivowitz* too has vanished?'

Sergeant Callan was turning red in the face, redder still beneath his tan, but he looked. The bottle was gone, nor was it to be found anywhere in the office.

'Perhaps you'd like to search *me?*' cried Guy Fowler, white with suppressed rage. He whipped off his flannel jacket, turned out his pockets, disclosing only a rather flattish but expensive alligator wallet, two or three gold-encrusted fountain pens and pencils, a comb, nail-file and handkerchief, some assorted keys and a dollar or so in small change. 'There!' he said. 'Though how anybody in his right mind could think a bottle that size could go in anybody's pocket—'

'But you knew about the bottle, and its size?' put in the Inspector.

104

'Of *course* I knew! Anybody who worked with Mr Karas knew that he nipped on his national beverage every once in a while. And besides—' Guy looked at Miss Withers—'I came in here this morning to see this lady sniffing the cork and I thought about to have a short snort, thought she put it out of sight fast enough. So I got a good look at the bottle.' He turned on Callan. 'All right, officer. So if I'm being accused of trying to murder Mr Karas—the only person in this town who'd give me even a part-time job when I needed it worst—then I demand my constitutional rights and I want to have a lawyer present—'

'Oh, shut up!' barked Sergeant Callan, not unreasonably. 'You were asked a couple of questions and I guess you answered them. Nobody is as yet accusing anybody of nothing, see? That's all from you for now. Siddown and wait until your statement is typed and then you can sign it and go.'

Guy Fowler sat, replacing his belongings in his pockets. After the brief statement was typed out in triplicate and he had read it at least twice, he went over to the desk and affixed his signature—somewhat callously, Miss Withers thought—with a dying man's pen. Then he left the room, slightly chastened.

'I just don't like the fellow,' Inspector Piper said.

Miss Withers sniffed a prodigious sniff at him. 'I thought that *I* was the one who's supposed to have the psychic hunches around here. And just because a young man speaks with a cultured New England accent doesn't necessarily mean he's the person for whom we're looking.' She turned to the sergeant. 'Honestly, I don't see how we can at the moment put Mr Fowler very high on the list of suspects; not after the ambulance doctor admits that it was Guy's finding Karas as soon as he did, and administering first aid, that gives the man whatever chance for life he's got. One doesn't put a rare poison in somebody's drink and then break one's neck to save him; it's not reasonable. Not,' she added thoughtfully, 'that much of this entire thing is really reasonable.'

'Oh,' said Callan. 'Thanks,' he added, not at all thankfully. He turned to the uniformed officer at the door. 'Bring in another one.'

Mr Ralph Cushak was next, obviously harried and just as obviously intent on being helplful and getting it all over as quickly as possible. He hastened to point out that he himself had never been in New York City except on flying business trips with the big boss; that he had no interest in the houris of show-business and that he had never heard of Zelda Bard. Questioned further, he was unable to say definitely about the whereabouts of any studio employee four years and more ago.

'They come and they go in this business,' Cushak explained. 'The movie cartoon field is a sort of closed shop; the three or four hundred creative people who work in it are always pushing for better jobs—they drift back and forth from Metro and Paramount's New York offices to the commercial cartoon outfits in Chicago and then back here to Disney's and Warner's and Lantz's and our own place, almost always the same people. It's a very difficult field for a young artist or writer to break into; you have to be a mixture of both and be a little crazy besides. We have a saying—"The business needs new blood; send us some and we'll shed gladly."' The only studio artist he was sure about was the late Larry Reed, who had been with the company almost from its inception and who had never taken any long trips except that last long trip into the Unknown. On second thoughts, Cushak seemed to remember vaguely that Janet Poole had had a year at the Art Students' League in New York, that Rollo Bayles had taken leave of absence once or twice to visit relatives and his mother's grave in Weehawken, that Tip Brown went back to New York every fall to catch the new shows . . .

'All of which proves little or nothing anyway,' Miss Withers pointed out. 'You both seem to accept the idea that Zelda Bard was poisoned by somebody in Manhattan. The poisoned brandy that came to her through the mails could have been sent from anywhere—even from the local

106

post office. Or Burbank, or Glendale, or any of the branches of the Los Angeles system.'

'Huh?' said Sergeant Callan.

'Jealousy is a terrible thing, and it can work long distance.'

The Inspector thought for a moment, and nodded. 'She's right on this, Sergeant. And the Bard girl had appeared all over the country in her act, vaudeville and burlesque and night clubs. She could have made enemies anywhere, and she was just the type to do it. We can't even be sure it's a man we're looking for; she could have stepped on a lot of women's toes, too.'

Callan nodded slowly. 'Could be a dame. They say dames tend to use poison when they want to get rid of somebody.' He turned to Miss Withers. 'What's that?'

'I said, "*You* too!"' she murmured. 'Forgive me, but I am rather up to here with *clichés*. Perhaps—' She stopped, and bit her lip. It was not the first time that she had been talking when she should have been listening.

'But,' said Mr Cushak suddenly, 'there's nothing actually to prove that the cases are related—Miss Zelda Bard didn't receive a poison-pen valentine, did she?'

'No,' admitted Oscar Piper. 'Not that we know of, anyway. There's no connection except that a very rare, hitherto unknown poison seems to have been used in all three cases. And it is likely to be used again right here in your studio unless something is done.'

Mr Cushak bit his lip. 'Then—then I've no choice but to close down the place, as of tomorrow night. We can't make funny pictures with this hanging over our heads. We don't want to lose any more of our people, and we can't stand any more of this publicity. You just don't know what certain newspapers do with anything that happens out here in Hollywood.'

'My heart bleeds,' said the Inspector unsympathetically.

Miss Withers spoke up. 'So you close down the studio and the murders never get solved. This new flare-up of the poison-ivy thing centres here, and here it must be resolved if anywhere. If you ask *me*, which I admit nobody *has*—'

'Excuse me,' interrupted Mr Cushak. 'I've got to go and arrange to bank the fires and put the place on a stand-by basis.' He looked at Sergeant Callan. 'Is it all right if I go now?'

Callan waved his hand. As far as he was concerned they could all go, and though he didn't say where, his attitude was clear. The sergeant was in over his head, and knew it. But as Cushak left, he nodded to the officer at the door to bring in the next one.

It turned out to be Joyce Reed. The lush, bumptious brunette had recovered from her earlier nervousness, Miss Withers noted. She turned her eyes on Sergeant Callan with obvious confidence; he was a man and she knew what to do about men. Joyce sat down, crossed her legs with a sort of maidenly immodesty, and waited.

She answered the preliminary questions without hesitation. Yes, she knew Mr Karas—naturally she knew him, through her job at the studio. She had never been out with him or had anything to do with him outside of business. She knew that he sometimes nipped on something alcoholic, because she had smelled it on his breath. She had no idea—

'What about your ex-husband, Larry Reed?' Miss Withers cut in. 'What were the circumstances of your divorce?'

'Larry? But I thought—'

'The cases are obviously related, my dear. Larry Reed is dead and Karas is dying, and we've got to put an end to this.' Miss Withers moved closer.

The girl shivered. 'I—I see what you mean, I guess. Well, Larry and I just didn't get along. I took all I could, and then—'

'Other women?' demanded Sergeant Callan.

'No!' Joyce said proudly. 'It wasn't *that* at all. Larry was sweet, but he was a born bachelor; he didn't want to be married, not really. When I wanted to go somewhere he'd insist on sitting home and painting things—hours on end he'd paint things.'

'And of course you objected to his gambling?' Miss Withers put in.

108

Joyce's big eyes widened. 'But he didn't, not that I ever knew of. He was very proud of his membership in the Society of Magicians or whatever they call it—he could do wonderful card tricks, but he always said that they had a house-rule or something which made it a point of honour not to play cards for money when they knew so many tricks. It wouldn't be fair, he said.'

'That,' said the Inspector, 'doesn't fit in with what we know about his valentine.'

Joyce shrugged. 'I can't help that. But while I lived with Larry I never knew him to gamble, and he'd only play bridge when I insisted, for a quarter a corner.'

Miss Withers frowned. There was a point here, if she could only put her finger on it. Something rang sour, like a cracked bell. 'I wonder—' she began.

'You can wonder later,' said Sergeant Callan. He turned to Joyce. 'You were pretty bitter about your divorce, no?'

'No,' said Joyce calmly. 'He's—he *was*—a very sweet guy, but no husband. We parted fairly amicably, and we sometimes had lunch or dinner afterwards, because we stayed friends. And if you're trying to suggest that *I'd* poison him . . .'

'Nobody suggested that,' put in Miss Withers. 'But somebody did, you know. We're just trying—'

'Okay, okay,' said Sergeant Callan, mopping his brow. 'Shut up, will you?' He turned back to Joyce. 'You got any idea of who might want to poison your ex-husband?'

She shook her head. '*Nobody* would. He played a lot of practical jokes and stuff like that, but it was all in fun. Nobody ever stayed mad at him—I certainly didn't. And I'll tell you, if it's any of your business, that if he'd crooked a finger I'd have come back and gone to bed with him any time after the divorce; I'd have remarried him any time if he'd promised to drop the paint brushes now and then to go dancing with me. He was a dear guy and sometimes, believe it or not, it's easier to get a divorce than to get rid of memories . . .' Joyce was crying again.

'But on the other hand . . .' began Miss Withers.

Sergeant Callan waved her down. 'That's all, Mrs Reed.'

'You mean I can go now?' Her eyes were shining.

'Yes, you can all go now!' Callan had had about enough. 'I'm getting so much help with this case that I can't hear myself think. Inspector, get in touch with me later, huh?'

Oscar Piper winked at him understandingly and then assisted the bristling schoolteacher out of the room. They made their way through the music stage with its rows of fretting people, and then paused at the main doors to look back. Janet Poole was being summoned into the inquisition —her shoulders squared and lips tight and bitten—for her turn at questioning. 'I would like to be there,' said Miss Withers.

'You were there, in spades,' Oscar Piper said. 'Vocally, too.'

'I was only going to suggest to the sergeant,' she countered defensively, 'that he ask some very pointed questions of one Rollo Bayles when the time comes.'

'Bayles? But you said he was a pip-squeak character.'

'Yes, and no. Bayles is the inhibited sort of man who could quite possibly love and then hate a woman—or two women. He could also hate the men whom he thought to be more successful with them than he'd been. He's all twisted up inside, like—'

'Like a pretzel?'

She sniffed. 'Never mind, Oscar. Perhaps sometimes I am talking when I should have been listening, but I was only trying to help the sergeant, even if he didn't want it.' They came out into the sunlit studio street, and each drew a deep breath.

'You mustn't mind Callan,' Oscar Piper told her. 'He's just a cop, trying to do his job, and a bit befuddled—that makes him touchy. He's naturally confused—'

'He's not alone in that,' Miss Withers said, with a sideways glance. 'Not that I really mind being given a brush-off just now; if this case is ever solved it will not be in that stuffy office, with that bumbling moron in charge. But Oscar, I'm really worried; the murderer is having things

110

entirely his own way, he's calling all the turns. If—' she added thoughtfully—'it is a he at all.'

The Inspector stopped short. 'Huh? What d'you mean? Outside of pretty office secretaries and messenger girls who don't really count in the picture, what shes have you got to suspect—unless you mean the Poole girl?'

'I don't know exactly what I mean, at the moment. But it's certainly within the realm of possibility that your Zelda Bard was killed by a jealous woman, and Larry Reed too. Karas could have been a smoke-screen to confuse the issue —as if it needed it. And it comes to my mind that at the time Janet happened to discover her poison-pen valentine she also happened to have a loyal friend and admirer at hand to hear her scream, and to testify later as to her shock and surprise. It could be—' She frowned. 'No, I'm going too fast. I have a phone call or two to make before I try to come to any final conclusions.'

The Inspector said that he had a fistful of cigars to buy before he went any further, and departed in search of the studio commissariat, promising to rejoin the schoolteacher in her office in a minute or so. It was twenty minutes at least before he appeared in her doorway, looking somewhat pleased with himself. He fended off the affectionate advances of Talley, found the most comfortable chair, and said, 'Hildegarde, I have news—'

'So have I,' said the maiden schoolteacher glumly. 'I finally got through my long distance call to New York. It was a call to a friend of mine in the bursar's office at Marksville University, in an attempt to find out just when Guy Fowler studied chemistry there.'

'Yipes!' said Piper.

'No Yipes. He didn't, not ever. Not even postgraduate work or summer school or anything. Marksville seems to be about the only school Guy failed to matriculate at and be kicked out of. Which brings me back to a distasteful probability—'

'So,' the Inspector said, 'you're back on the idea that it's a woman.'

'You men are all alike. To you, women are either god-desses or else tramps. But no woman is ever the "clear mountain brook" that Guy Fowler so fondly thinks his Janet is; he'll learn that the hard way one of these days. But I was just thinking that every one of the trick valentines had within it a singularly nasty dig, something out of the recipient's past that was buried and not generally known—and yet which might have been confided to a pretty girl over a few cocktails. Remember, every one of the three men immedi-ately involved in this case took Janet out for a fling when she first came to the studio, and I have noticed that some-times men talk very freely to a woman . . .'

'Some men never get a chance to; they can't get a word in edgeways,' said Oscar Piper, not without some bitterness. 'I only—'

'Yes, Oscar. I suppose you'll go on to say that I'm barking up several trees at once, like the man in the Stephen Leacock story who leaped on his horse and rode off in all directions. Part of it, I'll admit, is in sheer desperation. The studio is going to be closed down tomorrow; meanwhile, this is one of the very few times in my life when I have actually been retained to solve a murder. I want very much to succeed. I also don't want this nasty murder cycle to continue; there's no sense in waiting until everybody in the picture is dead and then to arrest the corpse, which seems to be the masculine procedure.'

The Inspector looked at her with exasperated fondness. 'You through? Because if you are, I have something for you. I too made a phone call. I called the hospital.'

'Karas is *dead*, then?'

'Wrong, Hildegarde. He's improving miraculously under anti-histamine injections; he's recovered consciousness and is officially off the critical list. Whatever he got in his bottle of *slivowitz* or elsewhere, it wasn't enough to do the trick.' Oscar Piper jabbed his cigar at her. 'See what that means?'

'Perhaps,' she said thoughtfully, 'he could have dosed himself, but—'

'Tie it up with the description of the man who paid

Lucinda Wersbeck's funeral expenses and left only his initials, undoubtedly phoney—'

'Yes, Oscar, yes. But we can't eliminate the other male suspects because of that description; it's a simple thing for a young man to make up as an older one, to grey his hair and pad his tummy and adopt a phoney accent. Though why anybody would have gone to all that bother, so long ago, I don't at the moment see.' She shook her head. 'Lucy's name was signed to the valentines and Lucy is undoubtedly dead. She may be the key to this whole thing, but I still smell red herrings somewhere.'

'Then *why* was her name brought into it?'

'When we find the reason for that we'll have the whole secret. But the nurse who took care of Lucy at the hospital remembered her as being singularly unattractive; I believe her words were that "the Wersbeck woman had a face like a meat-axe". Faces like that do not launch a thousand ships nor burn the topless towers of Ilium, nor do men commit murder for them. It just doesn't make sense.'

'Yes, but—'

'All you policemen are alike; you get a theory and stick to it, rejecting everything else. Take your firm belief that what has been happening here is linked with your precious Zelda Bard case—it may only be the work of an imitator of that earlier success. You see, one of my phone calls was to the Los Angeles Public Library, and I found that they happen to have on file in their medical section a copy of the pamphlet on poison-ivy published by Marksville University —a pamphlet all about the poison-ivy concentrate and the methods of producing it. Any one of our suspects could have chanced on it, and made notes.'

The Inspector nodded, looking glum. 'That throws it wide open. I might as well go back home.'

'And I might as well go back with you, wearing sackcloth and ashes, if something doesn't break before tomorrow night.' The schoolteacher tapped thoughtfully with a finger-nail at her rather prominent front teeth. 'But Oscar, I have a sort of hunch . . .'

'Well?'

'You know my methods, Watson.'

He grinned. 'Yeah, Hildegarde, I know too well. When the watched pot refuses to boil, you throw a monkey-wrench into it.' He looked at his watch. 'It's past time to be hungry, speaking of pots. Let's go see what's cooking in the studio restaurant.'

But Miss Withers shook her head. 'You'll have to excuse me for lunch today, much as I would like to eat on your expense account, if any. Take Talley with you if you like, and buy him the usual raw hamburger. I'm going to be very busy.'

He started, and looked at her suspiciously. 'What,' he said, 'do you know that I don't?'

'In this particular case, only a glimmering. But sometimes they say that in hunting a shotgun is more useful than a rifle.'

'How cryptic can you get?'

'Oscar, you'd be surprised. Run along, will you?'

The Inspector stared at her for a moment, shook his head, and then with a long-suffering smile bent down to snap the lead on Talley's collar and allowed himself to be dragged out of the office. At moments like this, he knew full well, there was nothing to be done with Hildegarde except to watch and wait and try to catch her if she stumbled. When she got that glint in her eye—

Miss Withers sat down at the drawing-board, switched on the light, and picked up a monkey-wrench. It was in the shape and form of a red pencil, but it was a monkey-wrench all the same. And if she threw it into the watched pot . . . There was an odd smile on Hildegarde Withers's face as she started to draw a picture.

CHAPTER 9

'The best liar is he who makes the smallest amount of lying go the longest way . . .'

—SAMUEL BUTLER

The coral-pink house on Mulholland Drive was grey and lonely in the moonlight as Miss Hildegarde Withers wheeled her little coupé into the driveway and turned off the ignition. For a long moment the schoolteacher sat there building up her courage. This was risky business, she knew full well; she hadn't even the flimsy excuse of rescuing an imaginary trapped cat this time if she was caught at house-breaking.

The Inspector would have no part of it, so she had left him to pore over his Zelda Bard files and come alone. On second thoughts it looked safe enough; there was no light anywhere in Larry Reed's house, and there was no parked car in the vicinity. She knew that, contrary to popular belief, the police do not always post an officer for several days at the scene of a murder; they hadn't enough available men. But she moved cautiously all the same, around the house to the patio and the french doors. A bit of work with a hairpin —more difficult now because she had only the beam of a pen-sized flashlight to guide her—and she was again inside.

Nothing was changed in that house of death. The silences were all around her. She found herself remembering the Edwin Arlington Robinson poem—'They are all gone away, the House is shut and still, there is nothing more to say . . .'

Only there was something more to say, and she intended to say it. The prize she sought still stood on the easel, but something—perhaps only an old maid's curiosity— impelled her to move through the house, looking and sniffing. Evidently the electricity had been turned off; the refrigerator gave forth noisome stenches from spoiled food when she opened it.

But there was nothing which she could recognize as a clue, not anywhere. The bed where Larry Reed had died was still rumpled and unmade; she had a momentary desire to set it straight and then prudently resisted it. She came back into the living-room, and turned to the desk. There were only bills, paid and unpaid; no personal letters, no diary, no nothing.

Larry Reed had not been addicted to writing, she gathered. Or at least he hadn't kept carbons of his letters. There was a little heap of address books through which she skimmed briefly—Reed evidently had got a new one whenever the old numbers got too obsolete. She found Janet Poole's name in most of them.

'"Our clear mountain brook . . .!"' murmured Miss Withers. She could not resist the feeling that Janet was the key to this whole thing, somehow. Janet was the person most likely to have learned the personal secrets of Larry Reed, and Rollo Bayles, and Mr Karas. And yet—

'Dear me,' said Miss Withers to herself, and moved toward the easel. Then she froze as she heard a car pull up outside, and a key turn in the lock. She hastily beat a retreat to the kitchen, and tried to make herself invisible behind a cabinet. This was something she hadn't bargained for.

Larry Reed's relatives or heirs or whatever, she decided. It certainly wasn't the police, or there would have been a fanfare of sirens; the authorities out here always advertised their coming well ahead of time, no doubt to make sure that there would be no burglars around when they got there.

Anyway, the schoolteacher was considerably uncomfortable, taking one thing with another. There was the sound of soft, almost furtive footsteps in the other room; they went on down the hall and a moment later came back again. The reflected glow of a flashlight showed momentarily.

Miss Withers would have liked to leap out suddenly and say 'Boo!' but held herself back, being even without a hatpin since she had come round to the California custom of wearing no hat. But the sounds in the other room intrigued her; eventually her curiosity got the better of her and she tiptoed to the kitchen door. At that moment there was the sound of crashing and tearing, and a dull thud.

She gasped audibly, and then was caught in the white glow of a flashlight, pinned down like a moth. A woman's voice exploded in the room. 'My God, it's *you*!'

'It is,' said Miss Withers, advancing. Her small flashlight reached out and limned Joyce Reed.

'Do you haunt houses?' the girl demanded, her voice shaking.

'From time to time. And just what are you doing here, young lady?'

'I—I had a reason to come. I still had my key, and there was something I wanted to get, if you must know!'

'*What?*' asked Miss Withers quietly.

Joyce came closer, looking confused and frightened and angry all at once. 'It's none of your business, but I happened to want *this*!' She showed it, and it was an album of photographs, against a background which even the schoolteacher in this light could recognize as Palm Springs. There was a young couple on the edge of a swimming pool, there was Larry Reed on a motor-scooter, there was Joyce looking lusher and lovelier than ever in a beach-chair . . .

'So I forgot to take this with me when I left Larry,' the girl said. 'But it doesn't have any value nor any interest to anybody but me now, so I came back to get it. Any objections?'

'No,' said Miss Withers softly. 'My objections are to your tearing up the water-colour I came here to get, which I see is missing from the easel. Why?'

'So I tore it to shreds,' Joyce said. 'The hell with that long tall cold blonde, in spades doubled and redoubled. I just couldn't resist the impulse.'

Miss Wither nodded. 'So she broke up your marriage?'

'Janet Poole? Perish forbid. Larry didn't even know her then. He just wasn't fitted for matrimony, that's all. I wanted children, and he thought they were a horrible responsibility or something.'

117

'But you stayed interested enough in him to resent his romance with Janet?'

'No! There wasn't any romance, and that's what I resented. Janet went out with him and teased him on and then never even kissed him; she's cold as a Christmas goose except for that musician of hers. Larry was impressionable; he was so terribly in love with her for a while, but she never even gave him the correct time! Who does she think she is, anyway? Larry was worth four of her silly Guy Fowlers with the stuffy accent; I bet she still supports him, too.'

Miss Withers ruefully surveyed the wreckage of the water-colour strewn in the fireplace, now beyond any reclaiming. 'I wish you hadn't done that,' she said. 'I had plans.'

'I'm sorry,' Joyce told her. 'Honestly. I didn't know it mattered. But as we say in the south where I come from, it "pleasured" me some to rip it to shreds. I did it, and I'm glad. But then, I'm just a crazy mixed-up kid . . .'

'Cliché me no more clichés.' said Miss Withers. 'Mrs Reed, who do you think killed your ex-husband?'

Joyce froze. 'I don't know. He never had a real enemy. Nobody could have wanted to kill Larry, not even me and at times I had more reason than most. It just doesn't make sense, any sense at all. It's as if—as if he got something meant for somebody else.'

'But those practical jokes—?'

'No. It was all in fun, and the people he pulled them on knew it and laughed just as much as anybody else after they got over the first shock. He was just as quick to lend them fifty when they needed it.'

'So we come out by the same door at which we came in, which is nowhere.'

'Yes,' said Joyce. 'Do you mind if I go now, and take my photograph album? I've got a boyfriend waiting outside, and I think he takes a dim view of my being sentimental over stuff like this.'

'I don't mind,' said Miss Withers. 'The only thing I mind is that this case gets more complicated by the hour, with no sense to it at all. And I have only tomorrow in which to solve it, since they're shutting down the studio.'

'And I'm going off salary,' Joyce admitted. 'Which I can't afford. If I can help in any way—'

'You've helped a lot, in reverse,' said the schoolteacher, looking at the ruined bits of the water-colour. 'That was to have been Exhibit A. Good night.'

They departed by their separate entrances, leaving Larry Reed's house lonely and desolate again. Miss Withers came home and prepared for bed, giving her hair its requisite one hundred strokes, and feeling no confidence whatever in the morrow. Unless her trap worked—

That morning the sun's slanting rays slid down a certain side street in West Hollywood, crept through a venetian blind and then awakened Miss Hildegarde Withers as no alarm clock could have ever done. She sat up straight in her bed—no, this wasn't either her bed, it was an uncomfortable pallet made on the floor behind the bed, and she ached in every bone. Her bed was occupied by a lumpy recumbent figure made up out of blankets and pillows, with a grey beret and an old transformation arranged on the pillow; it was a classic device borrowed straight out of Sherlock Holmes. (Hildegarde Withers was a self-appointed member of the Baker Street Irregulars, a group devoted to the memory of the greatest detective who never lived.)

But the trap hadn't worked. She had spread out her valentines, and left her window invitingly open, too. She gave out with a disappointed sigh, for this was the Last Day.

The maiden schoolteacher creakingly arose and put on a flannel robe; she gave her hair a lick and a promise and then went out into the living-room where she found the Inspector and Talley both sound asleep on the sofa in positions which could not have been particularly comfortable for either of them. Both were snoring gently, and Oscar Piper gripped a nasty-looking police-positive .38, which she prudently removed from his hand before she jogged his shoulder.

'Rise and shine, my two heroic protectors,' she said with some acidity.

Talley woke first and wagged his stump of a tail, staying exactly where he was. 'Sweet spirits of nitre!' murmured the Inspector. 'In the middle of the night, yet?'

'It happens to be all of seven o'clock in the morning,' she said firmly.

The little Hibernian policeman sat up, arranging his dishevelled shirt and tie. He yawned copiously. 'So it was a dry run and nothing happened. I could have told you. Well, I did my part—I stayed awake until after five o'clock and there were no intruders, nobody even tried to try the door.'

'So I gather. But why *not*, Oscar?' She shook her head. 'I was so sure—'

'Probably just because the murderer of Larry Reed is under wraps in the hospital, recovering from his own dosage.'

'Mr Karas? Stuff and nonsense. The trap didn't work because somehow the killer failed to be fooled at my attempt to throw the monkey-wrench into the watched pot, as you are always saying.' Miss Withers frowned. 'But it did seem so presumable at the time; the murderer knows that senders of poison-pen letters are traditionally supposed to send one to themselves, so he carefully refrained. And then when he did get one—'

'Maybe he's somebody not on your list?'

'Stuff and nonsense again. I sent my little missives to everybody involved in the case, hinting that I know all. He was supposed to make an overt act, as the saying goes.'

'So he didn't, or she didn't. You and your valentines. How about some coffee?'

But she wasn't listening. 'They weren't jingles. I think the poem I used will at least match in literary merit the composition of the original writer. May I quote? It went:

TO WHOM IT MAY CONCERN—
NOW WE END THE DANGEROUS GAME

120

DO A MURDER—TAKE THE BLAME
FACE THE MUSIC, SOUND THE DRUMS
LOOK OUT, KILLER, HERE IT COMES

and I signed it LUCY and ZELDA, just in case you're right in thinking that the cases are linked.'

The Inspector yawned. 'Maybe your drawings of the dying penguin weren't convincing enough?'

'What has that got to do with it? The guilty party would still get the idea that somebody was stealing his stuff, and close on his tail—or do I mean trail? Besides, I can trace as well as anybody, which is all that was required. The studio is full of pictures of The Bird, in every conceivable position.'

'It sounds nuts to me. Sending the things out broadcast—'

'Yes, I sent them—or poked them under the office doors —to everybody. To Mr Cushak, and Cassidy the janitor, and to Guy Fowler, whom you dislike so much because of his manners and his Boston accent; I even sent a valentine to my collaborator on the Circus Poodle story, the effervescent Tip Brown. I was trying to use the psychological approach, Oscar. The receipt of the valentine should have aggravated the killer into intending to eliminate me, as the one person who knew his guilty secret.'

The Inspector stared at her, shaking his head. 'And how, for heaven's sweet sake, would he know for sure who sent it? It wasn't as if you'd signed your name or anything.'

'If I'd signed my name,' she snapped back, 'the whole thing would have smelled like a rat, or worse. That's what I tried to get around by this subtle touch; I had Talley put a smudgy paw-print on each valentine, as if the page had been left on the floor and he had stepped on it accidentally. Everybody in the studio knows that I have a poodle around day and night and all over the place, so that should have led our murderer straight to me. Only it didn't.'

'Yeah. You slept on the floor and I sat up all night with a roscoe handy, and nobody came to the party. You and your bright ideas. What do we do next—surrender?'

'"One who never turned his back, but marched breast forward, never doubted skies would break . . ."—Browning. It was a good idea anyway, and if I knew just why it didn't work—' She nodded. 'But I have one shot left in my locker. When we get to the studio today—'

'Breakfast first,' the Inspector said firmly.

She came back to present reality with a start. 'Of course, Oscar. Would you like a slice of Persian melon and some eggs Benedict, with guava jelly on the side?'

'Yes!'

'So would I. But give me a moment or two to dress, and I'll put on the oatmeal.'

Resignedly, the Inspector ate his oatmeal and drank his coffee, two cups of which were not enough to make him alert. Miss Withers looked on him with some compassion, realizing that he must actually have kept awake in her protection most of the night, which at his age was something. But now he was coming all apart at the seams.

'I'm sorry, but I don't have any benzedrine tablets,' she said. 'I suggest, Oscar, that you go back to your bed in the guest room and knit the ravelled sleeve of care; there is no need for you to come out to the studio until later. The little ceremony I have in mind can't take place until late this afternoon anyway, if it takes place at all.'

'Don't I get any briefing beforehand?' He yawned copiously.

'You won't need it; things will happen as they happen and I very much want your reactions without your having any preconceived notions. The general idea is to fight fire with fire—in fighting artists you use art. See?'

'Dimly,' he confessed. 'Maybe you'll pull a rabbit out of your hat—with the hats you wear you could pull anything out—but at the moment I think this whole thing is a dry run, and how I'll justify my trip to the commissioner . . .'

'Sleep on it,' she advised. He yawned again, and submitted. Leaving him and Talley in the spare bed—Talley being a poodle who could take a nap anytime anywhere with anybody—and leaving the breakfast dishes in the sink with a reasonable conviction that they'd be there when she returned, the schoolteacher set out for the studio in her modest little coupé, thinking dark thoughts. It would have been so much easier for everybody concerned if the killer had only obligingly come forward and trapped himself by blasting the dummy planted in her bed! But this murderer was like no other she had ever run across.

When she did get to the studio, she found it a place of deepest gloom, the cloud centering over Cartoon Alley, Little groups of writer-artists, animations, filler-inners, cutters and sound technicians had formed here and there along the walks and in the hallways, soberly discussing the personal economic problems of a studio shutdown. Most of the secretaries were at their desks, calling one employment agency after another. Pretty little messenger girls hovered like birds gathering for migration, debating whether to take up car-hopping in a drive-in restaurant or to tackle a rivet gun at Lockheed or one of the other aircraft factories. Nobody was doing any work; the pictures in production were still-born and forgotten.

Miss Hildegarde Withers passed through all this feeling more than ever like an alien, a stranger in a strange land. Her problems were not theirs. Yet she had come to feel, in her few days here inside the gates, a certain real fondness for the people of Never-Never Land. It seemed impossible that Peter Penguin's laugh should be stilled, even temporarily—not when the outside world was starved for laughter.

But what to do about it? How could one go about finding one rotten apple in a big barrel—without over-turning the barrel? The identity of the murderer was almost as much a mystery now as in the beginning; he struck without reason or rhyme. No, he used rhymes enough, on second thought. But there was still no reason—

She climbed the stairs and went down the hall to her office, somewhat sick at heart. Times were few and far between when she actually was invited to participate in an investigation, and to fail now—

She sat down at her desk and stared at the wall, at the hundreds of whimsical drawings depicting the adventures of The Circus Poodle. The story-board was askew again—something that always rasped her nerves was any picture not straight on the wall—and she rose to set it right. Then with a start the schoolteacher realized something. On her first day in this office, after Mr Cassidy had removed Larry Reed's belongings and after this particular story-board had been hung in place, a poison-pen valentine had fallen out from behind it, addressed to Reed.

Then the murderer had put it there *later*, after Reed was dead! He had never intended to give Reed his warning—the snake had struck first and rattled later! That proved that the killer was somebody with free access to this and the other offices, free to dose a bottle of mineral oil and then make away with it, destroying the evidence. And it proved something a great deal more revealing. The Lucy thing was a hoax, as she had long suspected. It was purely by accident that Lucinda Wersbeck had died; it was by accident that four studio people had been riding as passengers in the rented limousine that killed her.

And the crack about Larry Reed's being a card-sharp—it lacked the barb of the other jabs, because all the evidence went to show that Reed had never played cards for money, and didn't even have a deck of cards in his house! The murderer had been improvising then, knowing that it wouldn't matter anyway because Reed would never read the jingle.

Miss Withers realized that she, the police, everybody, had been sucked into the act of a deft magician, who had effectively used the old device called misdirection. Things were not what they seemed; it was the right hand the audience watched and the left hand that did the trick.

'How red can our herrings be?' said the schoolteacher aloud. But there was no earthly reason why four people here in the studio should be singled out for death-warnings in the form of ridiculous poison-pen valentines or for death itself, unless—

124

There was but one possible answer. The murderer was acting with a dreadful logic of his own which only now she was dimly beginning to glimpse. The schoolteacher, faintly elated, considered it from all angles for a considerable time, spent half an hour with the telephone directory and ten minutes on two calls, hanging up with a faint smile on her face. Then she girded her loins and went across the street to Mr Cushak's office, where Joyce sat as usual at the reception desk.

'Is he in?' Miss Withers demanded.

'Yes, but—' Joyce rose suddenly. 'I'm awfully sorry about last night, and that picture. I was way out of line, and—'

'Don't give it a second thought,' the schoolteacher assured her. 'We'll just have to go around through a different door, and I have one in mind. Just be a good girl and see if you can get me into the Presence.'

There was, surprisingly enough, practically no wait at all. She found the studio executive at his desk, eating aspirins as if they were popcorn. He was, it appeared, a man beside himself and not liking the company much. 'I think my ulcers have ulcers,' he confessed.

She murmured something commiseratingly.

'You don't know the half of it,' he continued glumly. 'The big boss is flying back from New York today. Sharpening an axe, with designs on my scalp. And do you know I myself actually received one of these fantastic valentines yesterday afternoon? *Me!*'

'I wouldn't worry too much about that,' she started to confess.

But the man went on. 'The Los Angeles police are on our necks about the Larry Reed thing, which is now officially declared murder. They have officers digging into the files of the public library downtown, trying to find the names of anybody who signed out for the Marksville pamphlet on poison-ivy concentrate—'

'It will take weeks and prove nothing,' Miss Withers prophesied. 'The slip was probably signed Lucy—or Mr P. R. F.'

125

Cushak rubbed his aching head. 'And the local police have been tearing up the studio looking for the *slivowitz* bottle that disappeared. They practically accuse me and everybody else here of having spirited it away.'

'An empty bottle with the label soaked off is like any other bottle. It could have been disposed of by putting it among the other bottles of cleaning fluids in the janitors' cupboards, or in a trash can, or by hurling it over the fence into the Los Angeles river bed, where I've noticed that such dead soldiers are no rarity. The police are welcome to spend their time looking for it, which may keep them out of our way. Because we have work to do.'

'Work!' he echoed bitterly. 'Who can work around here? The wheels have stopped.'

'You might listen a minute,' she said. 'I have a sort of plan.' And she explained, in some detail.

'*No!*' he cried.

'Listen. If it works, as I feel in my very bones that it will, the studio won't have to close down tonight—though you may lose a valuable employee to the gas-chamber. It's really not difficult—'

'*No* again! If you think I'm going to be a party to any such mad, theatrical scheme as this, you're crazy.'

'But this is a mad, theatrical place, and a mad theatrical series of killings. I was hired to do a job and I'm sure the head of the studio would want you to give me all cooperation as long as there is the faintest chance of success. Of course you personally have nothing to fear?' She looked at him critically.

'*Me?*' He gasped like a fish.

'I was only asking. But I want to make a point that you and everybody else in the studio is under suspicion until this is cleared up. So I want a projection room and this equipment . . .' She went on to elaborate. 'I also want this list of people there at four p.m. each with a drawing of Peter Penguin in his or her own hand.'

'They'll refuse to do it, even if I did ask them.'

'They wouldn't dare to refuse the police, and besides a

refusal to cooperate in the test would be a confession in itself. Don't you see?'

Mr Cushak definitely didn't see, but he was no match for Miss Withers when her dander was up. 'After all, you can *say* the police insisted on it, can't you? At least I know a member of the New York City police force who would be willing to be quoted, so it wouldn't be an out-and-out lie. And I imagine the local authorities would go along with it too, if called upon. It can't hurt, and it may help.'

Finally Cushak gave in, and bowed his head. 'Very well,' he said. 'But you must still understand—'

'I wish I did, and intend to. And of course you'll be the first to take the test, as a sort of bellwether to the flock?'

'*Me?*'

'Yes, you. The whole thing would be pointless otherwise.'

'The whole thing, if you ask me, is pointless anyway. But I'll try, if you're making an issue of it. Though believe me, I never drew anything in my entire life. Believe it or not, I hate art—even cartoon art.' He rubbed his forehead, and took another aspirin. 'I like figures, figures that balance. That, madam, is a rare thing in this industry.'

'I can quite imagine, from what I've seen of it,' the schoolteacher admitted. 'Everything seems to me to be slightly off-key, though amusing and entertaining. But the main point is that you will set up the stage and have the things there this afternoon?'

Mr Cushak, obviously acting against his better judgment, said that he would. 'But when the big boss gets here—'

'I will cope with him when he arrives,' said the schoolteacher firmly. 'After all, he asked me to take this thing in hand.' She thought a moment. 'Actually when he asked me to take over it was only a scare and not a series of particularly nasty murders, I must admit. But the principle remains the same. I consider it a sacred trust.'

Cushak muttered something that sounded like 'My God!' But he nodded, with obvious resignation, and ushered her out of the office.

She crossed the studio street with her head held high and

127

her hat slightly over one eye, but with high hopes in her maidenly heart. When she got back to her own cubicle she found the phone ringing lustily. It turned out to be the Inspector at the other end, and for once in his life he got in the first word. 'Hildegarde, I couldn't sleep after all, so I got up—'

'Very sensible of you, I should say.'

'Listen, I just called the hospital and your Mr Karas is gone.'

She digested this. 'The poor man—and they said he was getting better!'

'Not gone dead, just gone. He flew the coop. Got his clothes and slipped out of the hospital when the nurses were changing shifts this morning.'

'No!' the schoolteacher gasped. 'But—but how could he, in that condition?'

'They say you recover from these allergy things very quickly, or else you die. But he was supposed to have been kept there several days more for observation, at least. Obviously the man's taken a powder.'

'Nonsense. Maybe he just doesn't like hospitals.'

'Nonsense right back at you, old girl. The man must have just taken a trace of his own poison as a blind—'

'Or maybe *slivowitz* is the antidote for poison-ivy?'

'—and he's getting the hell out of town, because he knows the thing is about to bust wide open. Cold feet, I guess. Anyway, I've alerted Spring Street. We'll pick him up. 'Bye, Hildegarde.'

'Wait, Oscar!' she cried. 'I want you out here. If you find Mr Karas you can bring him too. The ceremony is set for four o'clock.'

'Bye, Hildegarde. I gotta get downtown.' And he hung up.

'*Men!*' said Miss Withers, making it sound like profanity. Trust Oscar Piper to go off on a wild-goose chase when she had planned an important supporting rôle for him in her drama. Well, as she had said before, there were more ways to kill a cat then stuffing it to death with butter. She thought

128

a moment, then called a telephone number she had called before, and finally was put through to a very charming gentleman who listened, thought about it, laughed merrily, and said he would be glad to have a date with her.

'Cutaway and striped trousers?' he asked. 'Or a plain business suit?'

She thought the latter. She thanked him and hung up, then sat back in her chair, thinking long thoughts and being ever more sure that this—the wildest of her many hunches —was right. The whole trouble with the case was that in the beginning she had started off with the wrong premise. It was like Abraham Lincoln's court-room story about 'If you call a tail a leg, how many legs has a dog got?'—the answer being that no matter *what* you call a tail that still doesn't make it a leg.

Misdirection—a most effective use of misdirection. Well, two could play at that game. If her plan worked—

She looked up to see Joyce Reed in the doorway. 'May I come in?' she asked, and did. Then she sank into the comfortable chair. 'Well,' said Joyce, 'it's . . .'

'You mean you got one of the trick valentines?'

The girl blanched. 'That wasn't—yes, I did! I found it in my mail basket this morning. But how did you know? I didn't tell anybody!'

'Never mind; it's my business to know things.' Miss Withers hastily changed the subject. 'Then what did you come here to tell me if it wasn't about that?'

Joyce leaned forward. 'Janet Poole and her musician are getting married; they're eloping tonight!'

'Really!'

'Yes, Tip Brown just told me. He's all cut up over it, because for some reason he has a terrible torch for that blonde Polack. If you ask me, he hasn't lost much. I bet the proposal was like in the Peter Arno drawing in *The New Yorker* where the girl turns to the fellow in bed and says "Get up, you jerk; this is our wedding day."'

'My dear girl—'

'Oh, maybe I'm catty, but I'll bet that pair have registered

129

as Mr and Mrs Jones at half the auto-courts in the San Fernando Valley. So maybe it's high time they made it legal, but anyway it doesn't seem fair for them to get out of town in the midst of a murder thing when the rest of us have to stay and get nasty valentines—'

'I doubt if the police will let them go very far, under the circumstances. They can be held as material witnesses, if necessary.'

'That blonde could be held for a lot more than that!' Joyce stood up. 'I wouldn't put anything past her, not anything.' Having planted this news, and this small seed of suspicion, the girl moved to the doorway. 'I'm just sorry for Tip Brown,' she added. 'He just walked off the lot and I bet he's across the street at the Grotto hanging one on but good.'

'Oh dear! And I wanted him around this afternoon. Perhaps if some friend should go and rescue him—?'

'I'd be more inclined to hang one on with him if I went there,' Joyce told her. 'The way I feel.'

'*Well!*' said Miss Hildegarde Withers when the girl had gone.

CHAPTER 10

'Crime like virtue has its degrees;
And timid innocence was never known
To blossom suddenly into extreme licence.'

—RACINE

Miss Withers stood in the doorway of the dimly-lit, smoky little bar-restaurant, sniffed disapprovingly, and then went forward bravely and sat down on a stool beside the one and only customer. 'Good morning, Mr Brown.'

Tip was studying the two glasses before him, one small and one tall, as if trying to memorize their contours. He barely looked up. 'What's good about it?'

'Why—'

130

'The studio closes down today, and I'm on a week-to-week basis with creditors hovering. You have no idea what it costs to be a bachelor in this town.' Then he remembered his manners. 'Care to join me, Miss Withers. I know it's a little early in the morning for boilermakers—'

'I think not. But boilermakers—isn't that what the Polish people call "puddlers"? I seem to remember Janet Poole telling me that interesting fact some days ago.'

The round pink face turned towards her. 'Yes, ma'am.' Tip Brown looked, she thought, as if he had been drawn through a knot-hole. 'I suppose you've heard the news; Jan and her damn' musician are getting married—they're eloping.'

'Important witnesses leaving town in the midst of a murder investigation? I doubt if they'd get far.'

'Jan mentioned that when she kindly called to break the news to me,' he admitted. 'They were going to drive back to Hartford and visit that snooty family of his, but I guess they'll settle for waiting a few days and meanwhile honeymoon at the Beverly Hills Hotel or somewhere nearby—any place Jan can afford. And it's such a waste of a lot of girl on so little guy, if you ask me.'

She nodded sympathetically. 'And there's nothing *you* can do about it, young man.'

He shrugged. 'Except try to crawl into a bottle, as you think I'm doing. No, this is the last one. I came across the street to buy them a magnum of champagne to take on their honeymoon; it's the last gallant gesture I can make. I can smile like Pagliacci and keep a stiff upper lip and maybe get to kiss the bride—'

'Champagne as a wedding present? I shouldn't think that so suitable.'

'I hope he gets stinko and passes out and stays there,' said Tip Brown vindictively. 'All through the damn' honeymoon. I just don't like the guy.'

'Would you be likely to like any other man who was more successful with Janet than yourself?'

'Frankly, no.' He swung around. 'And the bucket-sized

bottle of champagne is sort of a studio tradition; we always produce that for anybody who gets married. Usually it's a chip-in deal, only this time I decided to do it myself. I wanted to do something, and I'm damned if I'll go buy a waffle-iron so she can make his breakfast on it. You see?'

The schoolteacher thought she saw. This unrequited love —but as the song had it, it did take two to tango.

'You'll get over it in time; not that that thought helps much now,' she told him. 'You'll find somebody else. Now take Joyce—'

'You take Joyce,' he came back. 'She's the kind of girl who promises everything with her eyes and then fights you for the courtesy good night kiss at the door. She hasn't got over Larry Reed, and probably never will.' He downed his slug, and chased it with most of his beer.

'Better make that the sublime, as Browning said,' Miss Withers suggested. 'We have a hard afternoon ahead of us, in case you haven't heard. And I understand that Mr Cushak is looking for you.'

'Yeah, as usual. "His Master's Voice." For two cents I'd quit and go over to Disney's or Walter Lantz; I've always liked Donald Duck and Woody Woodpecker better than this damn' Penguin.'

'These cartoon characters you draw and write about— they're very real and alive to you, aren't they?'

'Real as live people,' he said. 'And a damn sight more dependable.' Tip Brown arose. 'Well, it's back to the tread-mill. It's been nice seeing you.' He went out.

'You'll see me again,' said Miss Hildegarde Withers under her breath. 'And don't think you won't!'

The bartender came up to her and ostentatiously wiped the mahogany. 'Well, lady, what's your pleasure?'

She thought. 'A fizz-water and two aspirins, please.' He winced, but made no comment, and she sat there, back in her concentration. She was actually trying to write a script (without any real experience) for a one-act play that might still, she hoped, have at least a good curtain. But there

132

would still have to be a lot of what stage people called 'ad-libbing' and mostly by her.

It was by now lunch-time, so she paid her modest check and went back across the boulevard and into the studio again, heading towards the commissariat. It was not that she felt particularly hungry at the moment, but she felt that this day at least she needed to keep up her strength. She came into the big studio restaurant and immediately set eyes upon Janet Poole and her Guy holding hands at a corner table, at least metaphorically holding hands. They were floating. Miss Withers paused beside them for a moment. 'I understand that felicitations are in order.'

The happy couple looked up at her—they seemed a bit puffy and red about the eyes. 'Yes, thank you,' Janet said quickly. 'He gave in. We decided, after arguing about it almost all night. We're going to Las Vegas tonight to be married, if the police will let us out of town. Otherwise we have to have blood tests and things and wait three days.' She touched Guy Fowler's arm. 'My man thinks I need his protection.'

'I said as much some days ago,' Miss Withers reminded her.

Guy nodded. 'That you did. Janet convinced me that it's silly to wait.'

'It always was silly to wait, if the thing is inevitable anyway. The Japanese have a proverb—"The gods bind together at birth, with invisible threads, the feet of those destined to mate."' Her eyes fell on the vast bottle of champagne standing on the extra chair at the table, and narrowed slightly. 'Oh,' she said.

'Our first wedding present,' Janet confided. 'From dear old Tip.'

'A very nice gesture and no doubt well-meant—though I should think that lovers would be intoxicated enough on love alone.' The schoolteacher bent down to touch the wired golden foil on the mouth of the bottle, studying it as if she had never seen a magnum before—which in fact she hadn't. A genie in a bottle—a genie of hangovers.

'Sit down and have lunch,' Guy Fowler suggested. 'We're just picking on sandwiches because we were up most of the night and we're not hungry, but you can shoot the works. How about a steak—I'll pick up the tab!'

'Who'll pick up the tab?' Janet said to him softly, but Miss Withers's ears were sharper than most.

'No thanks,' the schoolteacher answered. 'You two have your lunch and I'll retire to a corner; I have things to think about. Around this place I eat little and drink nothing until our mystery is solved. Which just possibly may be this afternoon.' She took her departure, feeling slight twinges of envy at the look on Janet's face. It was the bride-look, smugly and placidly possessive, the look of a big-game hunter who has finally cornered his quarry and had it centred in his sights. And Guy Fowler, for his part, had had the faintly apprehensive and embarrassed expression of the groom in a funny-paper cartoon.

'What she sees in *him*—' the schoolteacher said to herself as she went on to a lonely little table in the corner, remembering at the same time that probably nobody else would ever understand what she herself saw in the Inspector, if you came right down to cases. 'Everybody to their own tastes, as the old lady said when she kissed the cow . . . *de gustibus* . . .' Anyway, Janet had made her choice, and she appeared to be a young lady with a whim of iron, like Alexander Woolcott's aunt.

Anyway, if her hopes and prayers came true, the question-mark that hung over the young couple—and over everybody else in the studio, for that matter—would be dissipated after four o'clock this afternoon, or she'd know the reason why. Miss Withers ordered soup and salad and just as she was finishing her tea and looking inquiringly at the grounds—not that she believed in fortune-telling actually—she looked up with a start to see Rollo Bayles seating himself across from her, looking rather like a retired zombie. He was, to put it mildly, in a state of jitters.

'Do you mind?' he said.

'Do I mind *what*?' the schoolteacher countered, with

reason. 'Certainly I don't mind your joining me, if that's what you're thinking of.'

'I just want to talk to you a minute, Miss Withers. They say you're here in the studio for just one reason—to try to solve the Larry Reed thing. I just heard from Mr Cushak about what you expect us all to do for your stunt this afternoon . . .'

'Do you object to submitting to the test?'

He stiffened. 'Not at all. Though I happen to be an artist, and not a cartoonist. I don't have much experience at tracing drawings of penguins or ducks or woodpeckers. What I want to say is this. You've made your mind up about who the murderer is, haven't you?'

'If I have, and I'm not saying, I'll still have to prove it.'

'But you're all wrong,' Bayles told her, with a certain vehemence. 'I know what you're thinking. Reed was a louse, granted. He hurt a lot of people with his so-called practical jokes. But he never pulled one of them on Janet. She didn't kill him or anybody ever. You don't know her like I do; she's incapable of anything like that.'

' "The clear mountain stream," ' murmured Miss Withers. 'No man knows what a woman is capable of.'

'Or maybe you suspect *me*?' he went on. 'I hardly knew Reed, and certainly had no motive to kill him.'

'If my theories are right, as they often aren't, perhaps the murderer didn't either,' said the schoolteacher. 'Truth lies deep down, at the bottom of a well . . .' She shrugged. 'But to come back to Janet for a moment, now that we are on the subject. She denies to me that she had ever been in Larry Reed's house, but she must have been—there was a partly-finished water-colour portrait of her on his easel.'

The man's eyes widened. 'Is *that* all? You obviously know very little about art and artists . . .'

'I used to paint china, young man,' interrupted Miss Withers, slightly annoyed. 'And I can tell a Holbein from a Corot, anytime.'

'Sure. But you evidently don't know that artists engaged in portraiture often work from memory when they are

135

especially interested in the subject as Larry Reed certainly was. I myself have drawings of Janet at home, but she never posed for one of them. He might have used a photograph, too. But if that's all you have against her . . .'

'That isn't *quite* all,' put in Miss Withers quietly. 'It isn't half of it.'

But Rollo Bayles was through. He bowed, and took himself off, evidently having changed his mind about having lunch today. So, Miss Withers thought, here is another young man worried about Janet, or pretending to be. Some women had the power to instil that sort of devotion.

She finished her tea, looked at the dregs without seeing any pictures or symbols except question-marks, and went back to her office. On the way she passed Janet's office. The door was open, and she caught a glimpse of Guy Fowler helping Janet bundle her belongings into paper cartons held by Mr Cassidy; the girl was evidently pulling up stakes for ever.

Art materials, pictures, papers, everything was being bundled into the boxes. 'She'll be sorry,' said Miss Withers, mostly to herself. 'People have roots like trees, and they can't pull them up without a considerable readjustment.' But she said none of this to the young couple, only nodding pleasantly in passing.

The Inspector arrived shortly after two o'clock, looking smug. He had Talley with him, on a leash, and the schoolteacher had to be greeted as though she had been away for a month of Sundays. 'You took Talley with you all the way into downtown Los Angeles?' she wanted to know, busily shaking paws with the demonstrative beast.

'He was hell-bent to go,' Oscar Piper admitted a bit sheepishly. 'He howled like a banshee when I started out and left him behind. And there was no extra charge for him in the taxi. The boys at Spring Street were a little surprised to see a fellow officer toting a poodle; you should have seen their faces.'

'I can imagine,' she said.

'We found Karas, by the way. Or the local police did. He

was at the Los Angeles municipal airport, trying to cash a cheque for passage to Mexico City.'

'Really? And did you take him back to the hospital?'

Piper shook his head. 'No, he didn't appear to need hospitalization, though he looks peaked, naturally. We brought him back out here, and Sergeant Callan and some of the LA boys are quizzing him in his office.'

'Mercy me! I suppose they'll have a confession any minute, with their rubber-hoses and bright lights and things.' Miss Withers gave a disapproving sniff. 'I'm surprised you people haven't picked up the cute Russian trick of putting a pail over the prisoner's head and banging on it until he loses his mind!'

'Oh, come off it. Third-degree stuff is out, these days. We're bringing out the former desk clerk from Forest Lawn to identify him as the man who paid for the Wersbeck woman's funeral and burial. That should cinch it. So what are you smiling at?'

'At the idea of Mr Karas being Mr P. R. F., if you must know,' the schoolteacher said, straightening her face. 'All the same, I'm glad Karas is here in the studio, because in the next hour or two—'

'You're still going ahead with that crazy idea?'

'I am, Oscar, if it's the last thing I do.'

'This killer is too smart—'

'Exactly. Too smart for his or her own good. All through this case we've made the mistake of playing someone else's game. Years ago when I was a little girl my father told me that when you get up before a concession at Coney Island or the circus or the county fair and a man wants you to bet your precious spending money on something, don't do it. It's his game, and he has a gimmick, and he'll win.'

'Yes, but—'

'But me no buts. Any killer, whoever he is, is ultra-vulnerable to suggestion; he can be forced into a situation where without knowing it he betrays himself—or thinks he has. I must have your cooperation, Oscar, and that of the local police too, if you can wangle it. It'll only take half an

137

hour or so, and if it works—' She frowned. 'I'm afraid I'm not going to be too happy about the way it works, if it does. Murderers are so often the people you like best. The Mark of Cain is a hard sign to see. But I am trying to force the issue; I think I have a gimmick of my own.'

He stared at her strangely. 'You actually think you *know* who it is?'

'I'm afraid I do, Oscar. Without a shred of any real proof, as yet. I'll name no names now, but I'll settle this thing this afternoon or—'

'Yes,' he interrupted wearily. 'Or else you'll go back to crocheting or painting china, which you have threatened before and never do.'

'*This* time I mean it. It is a mental challenge. Four o'clock, mind!'

'*Women!*' he muttered. 'I'm going out for a cigar.' Talley the poodle wagged his tail understandingly. 'Okay, you can go too,' conceded the Inspector. 'But no more raw hamburgers!' He snapped the lead on Talley's collar and went out of the door, pausing to say, 'Hildegarde, sometimes I think—'

'Sometimes, perhaps. But be back by four o'clock, and I think it would be well to have that nasty little pistol with you.' She relapsed into a medium dark-brown study. It was one thing to know—and another thing to prove it.

CHAPTER 11

'Se non è vero, è ben trovato.'
(If it is not true, it is well invented.)
—ITALIAN PROVERB

For all the understandable doubts he may have had, Inspector Oscar Piper at four o'clock was in the main projection room of the studio; a vast slanting room it was, with rows of big leather chairs facing a big white screen. It was lighted at the moment from overhead—a light that shone into the faces of the studio people who were coming in to take their places, all dubious about the whole thing. They had been invited—or rather commanded—and so here they were. They took seats, mostly sitting well apart. Each carried a sheet of paper.

Rollo Bayles was there, still unshaven and distrait. Cassidy, with eyes like olives drowning in a stale martini, smoking a cold pipe, hunched in the front row smiling his derisive smile and dreaming perhaps of happier days than this. Tip Brown, his face pinker than ever from the effects of the boilermakers he had had across the street, was chewing chlorophyll tablets and trying not to look at Janet Poole, who was as usual clinging possessively to Guy Fowler's arm and looking radiant in a sort of frightened-fawn way.

Sitting in the back row was Mr Karas, pale as two ghosts. He was momentarily free of supervision, though a man in a dark-blue uniform and a badge hovered near the exit door. It had taken some fast talking on the part of the Inspector to arrange that, and if the thing petered out into a fiasco as he was afraid it would, his embarrassment would be considerable.

But they were all here, even Mr Cushak with his lips tight as if they had been zippered together, and Joyce Reed beside him, wearing—perhaps in mourning—a black dress which did nothing to conceal her obvious charms. All the ones who were left were here, the Inspector thought. And the presence of Larry Reed was all about them. Their lives and their jobs had been thrown out of kilter by this last few days. It was most interesting for the Inspector to watch their faces and wonder which—and if—and why—

Maybe Hildegarde did have something up her sleeve beside her arm; she sometimes had in the past. But he had no hunches, as she usually did—they all looked fairly guilty on the surface, from where he sat. They were all frightened, alert, jumpy as Mexican beans. Maybe, he thought, that was part of the idea.

There was a rather long wait—or at least it seemed long

to the Inspector and no doubt to everybody else in the place
—and then Miss Hildegarde Withers made her entrance,
towing a smallish, dumpy man in his fifties, whom she
placed on the aisle midway of the projection room. He at
once took out a small notebook and a large silver pencil,
looking very official and dignified and important indeed.

'Three-fifths ham,' thought Oscar Piper. 'What in hell is
Hildegarde up to?'

Nobody knew, perhaps not even the schoolteacher herself.
But she scurried back up the aisle for a brief conference with
the studio projectionists, then back again to nudge Mr
Cushak into action.

'*Now*,' she said firmly.

He reluctantly arose, and went forward to face the assemblage. 'Fellow-workers,' he began, 'you all know why we
are here. This is not my idea—but I mean it is an effort to
put an end once and for all—I mean, our studio is in
desperate straits, and the series of incidents which have
threatened us all for the past few days are—I mean is—
something that has got to be put an end to once and for all,
if you know what I mean . . .' He trailed off.

'Yes,' said Miss Hildegarde Withers from the audience,
hoping to save him from being everlastingly lost amid his
own platitudes. 'About the pictures—?'

'Thank you,' he said. 'You may or may not know that
Miss Withers has been working here among us as a private
investigator, though I'm afraid she hasn't got very far—'

'Excuse me,' the schoolteacher interrupted. 'But I know
the name of the murderer, if you're interested. We're just
trying to prove it, and eliminate all the rest of you. Do go
on, Mr Cushak.'

There was a heavy silence. 'I think—' began Mr Cushak,
and then stopped. He nodded towards Miss Withers. 'Perhaps *you* could explain this better than I?'

'Who couldn't?' she murmured, and then stood up and
faced them all. 'Each one of you was asked to bring here
your own individual sketch or tracing made from a regular
studio model-sheet of Peter Penguin, the Bird who stars in

140

most of the movies, in the same general position as the drawings on the off-colour valentines which many of you have received.' The schoolteacher adopted her best class-room manner. 'Will you initial them please on the back, and then pass them forward so that they can be compared with the original?'

From the row behind her Guy Fowler laughed, a bit derisively. 'This is nothing but a silly farce,' he said. 'I've read enough criminology to know that you can't compare drawings or printing the way you can handwriting or finger-prints.'

'Perhaps you are in for a surprise, young man. Just do as you're told and may I have the attention of you all?' She raised her voice. 'We are lucky to have with us this afternoon Professor Ainslee, one of the most distinguished experts in the field of graphology and questioned documents—' She nodded.

The dumpy little man whom she had brought into the room rose and bowed gracefully, then subsided again with his pencil and notebook.

'Professor Ainslee believes,' Miss Withers continued firmly, 'that if the drawings of The Penguin are magnified a hundred times and projected on that screen side by side with the original (just as I have seen the police do with fingerprints and photographs of bullets) he can point out damning parallels in the strokes of the pencil or pen or crayon. He says that once a person has drawn or traced a certain picture or design he is practically always certain to trace it again in the same way—the lines over-lay each other, the picture is begun with the penguin's tail-feathers or with the tip of his beak—so that the would-be artist betrays himself with every stroke. Isn't that so, Professor Ainslee?'

'It is, absolutely,' said the dumpy little man, rising to his cue. 'I have proved it beyond the shadow of a doubt, in a hundred separate instances which I am about to combine into a book to be published in the fall, and which I think will revolutionize—'

'Thank you, Professor Ainslee,' the schoolteacher cut him off firmly. She faced the group. 'Now will you complete passing your papers to me, please?' Miss Withers started along the aisle, but the Inspector caught her arm as she passed him, and whispered a puzzled query.

'Hildegarde, how much of this if any is on the level?' he demanded. 'In my work I've come to know or know about most of the famous graphologists, and I've never heard of this guy Ainslee.'

'There is much that you haven't heard of, Oscar. "There are more things in heaven and earth," unquote. Shakespeare. Sit tight, and keep your fingers crossed.'

She started on, then paused. 'Or better still, go get me a cup of coffee from the vending-machine in the hall; I'm a little faint with tension and excitement.' She smiled at him, and went on down the aisle.

He muttered something about 'Judas Priest in a revolving door . . .' but rose to obey, discouraging the poodle. It was Hildegarde's show, and he would go along with the gag—he had to.

The schoolteacher was going blithely down the aisle, collecting the various sheets of drawing-paper. As she came to Guy Fowler, the young man hastened to affix his initials on the back with the ball-point pen he had borrowed from Janet, returned it to her, and then held out their two drawings with a quizzical smile and a lifted eyebrow. 'I am one to go along with a gag,' he said.

'How nice of you, since you have no choice,' the schoolteacher reminded him. 'That policeman at the door isn't here just for fun, you know.'

'I know,' he said. 'Tell me, Miss Withers, is this clambake of yours going to take very long? We were hoping to make it to Las Vegas tonight.'

'Wedding bells to ring out?' She shrugged. 'There's not much I can do about it, but I'm doing what I can. I'm really as much in a hurry as you are, though for different reasons.' And she went on, not without a certain sympathy.

Mr Cushak handed her a drawing only faintly recogniz-

142

able as The Bird, with an apologetic shrug. Perhaps, the schoolteacher suddenly thought, it would be possible for the guilty person to have drawn as *badly* as he could—as much unlike the original as possible. But of course that in itself would be an indication . . .

And there was still that last shot in her locker, her own pet gimmick on which she pinned her last desperate hopes. She went on down the aisle, feeling somehow as if she were collecting examination papers—as in a way she was.

Tip Brown had characteristically drawn his dead Bird with the beautiful dexterity of the practised cartoonist; he had drawn it lying there with one eye closed in a rakish wink, obviously only playing possum. Rollo Bayles had painted his with a fine water-colour brush and with a faint suggestion of a scenic background. Joyce Reed had produced a meticulous copy, done in faint, uncertain lines. Surprisingly enough, Cassidy's offering was an artistic triumph, in full colour; he must have picked up a bit of art during his years around the studio, she decided. And even Mr Karas, worn and wan and far from his usual self, had prepared a drawing of sorts. 'It is not very good,' he apologized. 'My hand shakes today, and besides I am a musician, I am not a cartoonist.'

'It will be good enough for our purposes,' she told him. She started away, and then turned back, lowering her voice. 'Would you mind telling me why you left the hospital without being discharged, and why you tried to leave the country—just for the record?'

'Not at all,' he said. 'Somebody was trying to kill me. And I don't trust your hospitals; I don't like Hollywood or your United States. I wanted to get away. Is there any law that says I can't?'

'There is a law against murder,' Miss Withers told him bluntly. 'In case you haven't heard. And there is a law which says that material witnesses can be locked up and held for weeks or months, in case they show signs of wanting to disappear. If you are held, I will, however, be glad to

143

send you cheery postcards.' Karas subsided unhappily, and she went on.

With all the drawings finally in hand, she hastily numbered them in the lower right-hand corner, making a record on a slip of paper for her own fell purposes. She then took the batch of drawings to the projectionist, who said, 'Yes, lady,' in a weary voice before she had half finished giving him his instructions.

'Well, do it,' she said. 'I imagine you have a personal interest in seeing that the studio doesn't close down tonight?'

'Yes, lady,' he came back. 'I gotta family.' He said it almost sadly.

'Well, then. I'd like some cooperation.' And she told him.

He nodded. 'But it'll take a little time.'

'Very well, but hurry. I don't know how long I can keep them here.' She left the projection booth and came back into the auditorium. Her cup of coffee rested on the arm of her seat, and there it remained, untouched. They all sat there, like an audience waiting for an opening curtain at a play that is mysteriously delayed. Nobody spoke, nobody moved. It was the atmosphere for which Miss Withers had hoped; it was a place of worry and tension.

And then a light appeared on the control panel. The schoolteacher pressed the go-ahead button and a moment later the auditorium lights gradually faded into what seemed an inky darkness in which you couldn't see your hand before your face. Why, Miss Withers thought, would anyone want to see his hand before his face? Then suddenly on the big screen before them appeared the original poison-pen drawing of the dead Bird, more atrocious and obscene now than ever since it was magnified to the dimensions of a giant ostrich. What sort of mind, the schoolteacher wondered, could think of strangling Peter Penguin? It was like stabbing Tinker-Bell. The picture on the screen moved over to the left, and stopped.

'This is Exhibit A, Professor,' she spoke up. 'It's from one of the original valentines, by the hand of the murderer. The next picture will be from one of our test drawings.' She pressed the button again, and suddenly drawing number one appeared on the right side of the screen. There were two enormous dead penguins illumined—two sketches, but were they identical in technique? It was beyond Miss Withers to decide.

It was Mr Cushak's drawing on display; magnified, it looked like something done by a six-year-old child. 'Very interesting,' came the professor's voice. 'Hold it, please.' The projectionist held, echoes of dead, lost laughter filling the room. 'Lights,' said the professor, and the lights came on. He wrote very busily in his little notebook. 'Next, please.'

Miss Withers pressed the go-ahead button again, and again they were in darkness thick as pitch. Another drawing replaced the first, sliding jumpily into place beside the master picture. It was Joyce's the schoolteacher recognized, and no professional job either.

'Amazing!' said the professor. 'Lights, please. It reminds me of one case I had in Stockholm . . .'

'Next!' prompted Miss Withers, a little desperately. 'I mean—' She suddenly realized that she had to press the button, and did so. The room was in utter darkness again. And the cup of coffee remained on the arm of her seat; it was another invitation to the murderer, or was supposed to be one. She would have died rather than drink that coffee; if her suspicions were right she would have died if she drank it. One could only hope.

Meanwhile the proceedings went on, with drawing after drawing displayed briefly on the screen. Meanwhile the professor was hamming it up, interrupting the affair to discuss handwriting and its allied fields, and dragging the ceremony out *ad infinitum*. 'I could *strangle* that man,' the schoolteacher whispered, still waiting.

At the next break Mr Cushak came up to her, looking worried. 'Perhaps I shouldn't mention it now,' he said almost apologetically, 'but just how much is this famous professor of yours going to cost the studio—I mean his fee?'

'I think its seventeen-fifty,' she whispered back. Mr Cushak almost swooned. $1750 was a lot of money, even if

145

it was somebody else's money. Cushak went away, looking most unhappy.

'I meant seventeen dollars and fifty cents—' she sent after him, but too late. Everything was too late at the moment. The party was going to hell in the proverbial handbasket— and the murderer somewhere in the audience still sat on his thumbs, in spite of all the attractive baits she had laid out.

Nothing worked right. The watched pot still refused to boil, even with all these monkey-wrenches (*spanners*, as our English cousins say) thrown into it.

The schoolteacher turned to Oscar Piper beside her. 'Why doesn't something happen?' she demanded.

'Because,' he confided, 'you're barking up seventeen wrong trees all at once. I take a dim view of this whole thing, and always have.' Which was no comfort.

So the session went on and on interminably, the professor taking longer and longer to study the exhibits, and making longer and longer notes during the period when the lights were on between exhibits. He also seemed to have an irresistible tendency to make little speeches about his previous experiences in the field of graphology. Miss Withers usually managed to cut him off with a polite firmness which got thinner and thinner.

The group, the captive audience, grew more and more restive. They went out for drinks, for coffee, for cokes. They drifted hither and yon, but nobody drifted out of the picture; the officer at the door saw to that. But they were all seemingly bored with it all; there was a very real question in Miss Withers's mind as to how long they could be held here under her extremely moderate authority. And then somebody—a smallish man in sports shirt and slacks— came to sit down beside her.

'If you don't mind—' he began.

'I do very much mind,' she snapped. She had noticed him hovering in the background for some time, a jollyish, frivolous-looking man who rather resembled a shaved Santa Claus. 'I'm busy, and nothing works, and they're all about to walk out on me.'

146

'No, ma'am,' he told her. 'They won't leave if I say not to, only we try not to do things around here that way; we like to think it's one big happy family.'

She did a double-take. *'What?'*

And the man introduced himself. 'I just got in on the plane half an hour ago, and I guess it's high time. I just talked to Cushak, and he told me what you're up to.'

'Oh, heavens!' the schoolteacher was flustered. 'I suppose you think—'

'It's not such a bad idea, really,' he interrupted. 'This party, I mean. Maybe it isn't going as badly as you think. If you don't mind one small suggestion—'

'I'm afraid it's too late for that,' Miss Withers said mournfully.

'Maybe not. But this is what occurs to me.' And he told her.

'Good gracious!' She set her coffee cup down on the aisle, so that she could lean closer to the big boss of the studio, the man behind the men behind the pencils and brushes and cameras. 'I thought I noticed everything, but that escaped me. You mean only four fingers, *always?'*

'Four fingers,' he repeated. 'Counting the thumb. We don't know where it started, exactly . . . maybe back with Disney's *Steamboat Bill* or before. But you look at Woody Woodpecker or Donald Duck or any other cartoon character. It's a solid tradition in the business. None of us would ever dream of doing it otherwise.' He sat back placidly and lighted a cigarette. 'You take it from here, lady. You're doing all right—and I don't think we're going to have to shut down, after all.'

The lights came on again as the professor finished another of his monotonous dissertations, and the schoolteacher started to rise. Then she suddenly noticed that Talley the poodle, who had interested himself in her coffee cup in the hope that it might hold cream and sugar, was busily kicking imaginary dirt over it, in the ancient canine gesture of disgust and revulsion.

'So!' said Miss Withers. She picked up the cup and handed

147

it to the Inspector. 'But don't drink it,' she hastily added. 'Save it for analysis.' Then she girded her loins and went down the aisle to where the professor was still gallantly stalling for time—if ever a man earned his $17.50 it was this one.

'Cut,' said the schoolteacher. She took the centre of the stage, with considerably more confidence. 'Good people, the party's almost over,' she announced. 'You can all go home —except just one of you, of course. I mean the murderer, the original sender of the poison-pen valentines, who made the mistake of drawing Peter Penguin with *five* fingers, when everybody who has ever worked in the film cartoon field knows that it's a tradition to draw only four.'

There was a frozen silence in the room. 'Our murderer,' Miss Withers continued carefully, 'was a person who had moved in and used the studio and its facilities and conventions for his own foul designs—but he didn't know that one thing. However, he knew a lot of other things; he knew for instance that the field of murder investigation is full of truisms. The murderer is always supposed to return to the scene of his crime, poison is a woman's way, and writers of poison-pen letters always send one to themselves. To quote Mr George Gershwin again, "It ain't necessarily so."'

She paused, and the Inspector came up beside her. 'Let's give up, and go home,' he suggested. 'You aren't getting to first base.'

'Hold on to your hat, Oscar.' She turned back to the assemblage. 'In this case, we have a murderer who *knew* all these clichés, these truisms, and who took special pains to do the exact opposite. He *didn't* return to the scene of the crime, and he used poison though he *wasn't* a woman, and he *didn't* send a poison-pen valentine to himself—though he eventually got one, concocted by myself, and that resulted in the overt act of putting a bit of the poison into the coffee-cup I'd left handy. Since you are all involved, and your jobs are at stake, I'd like you to see it for yourselves.'

She went back to the control table and pressed a buzzer. 'Can we have number six again?' she asked.

'In a minute, lady,' said the projectionist through his little porthole.

'It makes no sense—' Tip Brown began, restively.

'It certainly doesn't!' put in Guy Fowler. 'How long does this go on? Janet and I still want to get to Las Vegas tonight, and do we have to listen for ever to this claptrap? It's almost five o'clock.' Jan shook her head and tried to pull him back into his seat, but he shook her hand off and stood erect again. 'Well?'

'You aren't going to Las Vegas, or anywhere,' Miss Withers told him coldly. 'Watch the screen.'

The lights went out again, and again there were two drawings of the dying penguin, side by side. 'The original poison-pen valentine and the replica,' said Miss Withers. 'Both of the drawings you see are Mr Guy Fowler's, and both have certain interesting variations in the fingers. Too many, for cartoons—for Never-Never Land. I have it on excellent authority.'

Back came the lights.

The room was gelid. And then Guy Fowler broke the stiffness by coming up the aisle, his face stiff and ugly. 'All right,' he said. 'When I was practically forced to draw a picture of a dead penguin I drew it with five fingers instead of four. How silly can anybody get? Try making something of that in court.'

'Everyone else in the place knows the conventions about cartoon characters' fingers,' said Miss Withers softly. 'I could never really believe from the beginning that this was really an inside job—nobody who had ever worked on Peter Penguin would possibly conceive of drawing him dead; he's as immortal as Mickey Mouse or Popeye the Sailor. The valentines were drawn by somebody who had complete access to the studio, but who didn't know all the rules. You, Mr Fowler.'

He still came forward, and in such a manner that for the first time in his doggish existence Talleyrand the poodle stood up and growled at a human being. 'So you're trying to make *me* the patsy,' Guy Fowler cried. 'Just because I drew too many fingers on the penguin.'

'And there were too many fingers on the dead penguin in the original valentine,' Miss Withers reminded him.

There was still fight in him. 'So *I'm* supposed to have killed Larry Reed, a man I hardly even knew?'

'But he was a man who had played a rather rude practical joke on you, as he had on many others, so you disliked him enough not to care particularly whether he lived or died. And it appears that you didn't care much for Mr Karas either, even though he'd been kind enough to give you a part-time job at music arrangement. You knew about Larry Reed's hypochondria and his bottle of mineral oil that he kept in his desk; you knew about Mr Karas's bottle of *slivowitz*. Easy places to plant poison, I should think. As in my coffee cup just now—because you knew that I knew. You thought you'd covered yourself by discovering Mr Karas in the wash-room and giving him first aid—but it was all part of that phoney pattern you'd tried to assemble, the one you luckily hadn't yet quite time to accomplish.'

The schoolteacher advanced towards him belligerently, and Guy Fowler backed away, not entirely from the effect of Talley's growls.

'I saw you come up the aisle in the darkness,' said Miss Withers. 'It's an old trick, really. I kept my eyes shut when the lights were on, and so in the darkness I could see you deftly dosing my coffee. We'll hold that for the police laboratory people. You're gone, young man.'

Guy Fowler seemed to shrink, suddenly. 'I want a lawyer,' he said.

'You can have ten lawyers,' said the schoolteacher. 'But it will all come out. They can perhaps make it sound preposterous—taking the life of a fellow human-being is never sensible any time—but the facts are the facts. You were a would-be pulp writer a few years ago, and possibly this is your supreme achievement. But the whole thing, the murder of Reed and the attempted murder of Karas, was a blind, wasn't it? Just because four people happened to be in a car that happened to hit a girl you never knew?'

Guy Fowler reeled back, his mouth working. But no words came out.

'You were building all this thing up, with the valentines and all, to cover the fact that you wanted to kill Janet—weren't you?'

He froze, standing in the aisle. There were no words to say.

'You thought, young man, that you could conceal one murder underneath several others, all linked to a completely phoney premise. We were supposed to hunt for an imaginary Lucy or for a boyfriend of hers just because of an accident which was purely that and nothing else, a link in a nonexistent chain. It all was leading up to your real murder, the one you haven't yet had quite time to accomplish. Though I imagine you'd have managed it quite neatly, perhaps with the help of the the magnum of champagne which you'd have made sure that Janet drank—'

'Oh, *no!*' said Tip Brown, coming forward.

But Janet had fainted, collapsed in a huddle under her seat.

'Prove it—prove any of it!' challenged Guy Fowler. 'My family's lawyers will tear this apart in a minute—'

She smiled, a mirthless smile. 'Your precious family—and your precious first wife whom you thought might take you back into her arms now that you're starting to be a successful song-writer with your *Meditations on a Melting Icicle* or whatever the title is! It won't work, young man.'

He said nothing. Mr Cushak arose, obviously worried. 'I don't think this is really getting anywhere, and—'

'Oh, shut up, Ralph,' said the studio boss. 'Go back and sit down.' He nodded to Miss Withers. 'Say it all, ma'am.'

'I'll try,' said the schoolteacher. She turned back on Guy Fowler. 'You wanted to go home in triumph, didn't you? But Janet Poole, the girl from a Polack family south of the railroad tracks, couldn't possibly fit into the picture. Yet you'd borrowed a lot of money from her and lived on her and registered at hotels with her; maybe you even went through a wedding ceremony with her in Tijuana, though that sort of thing has no legal hold. Anyway, she was easier to get than to get rid of, wasn't she?'

He gulped like a beached fish.

'We might as well,' continued Miss Withers, 'clear this up here once and for all. It will perhaps be hard to prove that you sent poisoned brandy to Zelda Bard through the mails, though under the circumstances it is quite possible to believe that some years ago you fell in love with her, as college boys often fall in love with glamorous Broadway dancers, who unfortunately have a tendency to lead them on a little and then say No. It will be hard to prove that you put the poison-ivy concentrate into Larry Reed's bottle of mineral oil, or into Mr Karas's bottle of *slivowitz*, or just now into my coffee cup! Perhaps I've done you an injustice, Mr Fowler—'

· Tip Brown had Janet up in the seat again, and was chafing her wrists. 'Let her stay out for a few minutes,' recommended the schoolteacher. She turned back to Guy. 'I will be glad to give you an apology, and sign it with a flourish, if you'll just lend me your fountain pen.'

He looked inches smaller. 'What—*what* did you say?'

'I mean,' Miss Withers said, 'the big gold-encrusted fountain-pen that you've always carried and never used, to my knowledge. You *didn't* use it signing your statement to the police in the Karas investigation, you *didn't* use it for initialling your drawing of the Penguin today. Why not? Unless there is something in it instead of ink—such as poison-ivy concentrate, perhaps? Do you mind if we look?'

Joyce Reed suddenly started to laugh, and then cut off as she saw Guy Fowler's face. The handsome young man was trying hard to smile a withdrawn, derisive smile, but he had suddenly come all apart like a puppet loosed of its strings.

'Curtain,' said the studio boss to Miss Withers. 'Cut, and print it.' They all watched in a sort of paralysed horror as Guy Fowler tried to throw away his fountain-pen, tried to run for the door, tried to become invisible. He fell down, he drooled and slobbered.

'I'm glad,' Miss Withers thought, 'that Janet fainted.'

CHAPTER 12

'. . . The mental spasms of the tortured Cain . . .'
                                    —WILLIAM E. AYTOUN

There was really nothing left of Guy Fowler now, no real resistance at all under the firm pressure which Inspector Oscar Piper applied, professionally and mercilessly. Guy had run out of lies, he had run out of pretence, he had run out of pulp-magazine fiction and had sent his last valentine. He talked, he talked there in front of them all, a spate of ugly words . . .

It was not a happy scene, even though it ended the whole thing in a way which Miss Withers had feared. She was glad to see the man taken away at last by the local policemen, hopelessly involved in his own lies and not even now counting on his family's lawyers.

'We got him cold,' said Oscar Piper. 'With that fountain pen . . .'

She nodded. She nodded again as the head of the studio shook her hand and said nice things, as Mr Cushak made apologies, and as the others gathered around to voice their thanks and relief.

'So we don't close down,' said the boss. 'Understand, everybody? Back at the treadmill at nine o'clock tomorrow morning. Peter Penguin rides again.'

The studio people slowly started to file out of the projection room. Mr Cushak put in his five cents. 'You heard the orders,' he said. 'That's nine, and not nine-thirty or ten, understand? We have lost time to make up.'

Somebody made a vulgar sound, no telling who. But the heat was off, and they all felt like laughing, even if a little worn by the afternoon. And Peter Penguin would be laughing too tomorrow morning, laughing again on thousands of movie screens for months and years to come, eternal laughter which somehow couldn't be stilled by the machinations of one deluded young man who had crowded into the picture and used it for his own purposes and now would probably be crowded into the death-chamber at San Quentin—unless the local authorities gave him up for extradition. 'It's six of one and half a dozen of the other,' said Oscar Piper. Anyway he had his confession, taken down on a wire-recording by studio sound-men. The Zelda Bard case would go into the Closed file the moment he got back to New York, and the thoughts gave the wiry little Hibernian a certain grim satisfaction.

He and the schoolteacher came out into the studio street, into a chilly dusk. 'Buy you a hamburger somewhere, Hildegarde—just to celebrate?'

'No,' Miss Withers said firmly. 'You're on an expense account, and you'll buy me dinner at Larue's. They say you can get a nice steak there for seven dollars. And I think I've earned a nice steak.'

They were driving down Sepulveda Boulevard towards the Los Angeles municipal airport (which isn't in Los Angeles) some hours later. The two old friends had joined forces in so many murder investigations—and from the very nature of things could hardly expect to join in many more. The sands were running through the glass, and they both knew it.

'Thanks for coming out,' she said.

'You're welcome—though I didn't do anything to help except fall over my own feet, I'm afraid.' He stiffened. 'Watch that truck!'

'Why? It's not doing anything interesting.'

'I am impressed enough with your recent triumphs to keep my mouth shut about your driving, but it takes an effort,' the Inspector confessed. 'That's a red light, in case you didn't notice.'

She stopped, half-way across the intersection. 'Poison-ivy concentrate in a fountain pen—handy at all times. It was a fantastic thing, Oscar, contrived by a fantastic mind.'

'Sure. Too smart for his own good. Remember Loeb and Leopold? The guy's family will come to the rescue with a horde of expensive lawyers, and he'll plead not guilty and not guilty by reason of insanity and a lot of good it will do him. The light is now as green as it will ever get, Hildegarde.'

She lurched ahead, thinking of other things. 'It was there all the time, Oscar. If I'd had the wits to see it. I mean the truth about Guy Fowler. He'd committed one successful murder four years ago, using an original technique. He killed a glamorous dancer who flirted with him a little and then laughed at him when he got serious, using the particularly sneaky technique of mailing her a Christmas present of poisoned brandy. He'd drifted out here to Holly-wood and managed to get himself deeply involved with a girl he didn't mind using and borrowing money from, but whom he considered beneath him. He couldn't pay her the money she'd advanced, he couldn't square it by marrying her because that didn't fit in with his desperate desire to go back home and show off as a success to his precious family . . . they'd never approve of a Polack peasant, or so he thought. Though she was seven times too good for him. Perhaps he had thoughts of getting back his first wife and her millions. A most devious mind, Oscar.'

'Some people are like that. Not many, happily. 'That's a boulevard stop, by the way. I only mention it in passing.'

'I'm afraid I've already passed it.'

'You have. I'm thinking that this whole thing is tough on the girl.'

'Janet? Of course it's tough. So is *she*—and maybe you noticed that it was Tip Brown who picked her up when she fainted, and who later carried her out of the place and comforted her as much as anyone at such a time could be comforted. They speak the same language, and he adores her, and I think that after she catches her breath she'll fall into his arms and be very happy there too. Any dog is allowed one bite, and any girl is allowed one mistake.'

'You and your quest for happy endings,' said the Inspector, grinning.

'Yes, Oscar. And one more thing—I don't want you to go back to New York without knowing about Professor Ainslee. His real name is something else; he's an ex-actor who agreed to play the part for me, at regular Screen Actors' Guild rates. He is also a field-man for the Motion Picture Relief Fund; he was the middle-aged man with the cigar and the accent (all actors have accents, and most of them, particularly those of his vintage, cultivate English accents) and as part of his routine duties he paid the costs of burial at Forest Lawn for poor Lucy—Lucinda Wersbeck, who had once been a motion picture extra and thus was entitled to this last gesture.'

'Mr P. R. F.' said Oscar Piper.

'Exactly.'

'I'll be everlastingly damned,' said the Inspector.

'I doubt it. But you must admit that he earned his regular fee of $17.50 for this afternoon's performance, and I have a feeling that, in spite of his having hammed it up considerably as we say out here, he'll get a job at the studio being the voice of Charley Crocodile or something. He made an excellent impression on the powers that be.'

They had parked the little coupé by this time. Inspector Oscar Piper hurried into the airport office, and then came back to her. His plane, whose motors were humming and which was obviously about to get going, stood neatly on the runway.

'Well,' said Oscar Piper. He hesitated, and then on a warm Irish impulse he reached over and kissed the school-teacher full on the lips. 'There's your gold star for merit,' he said, and rushed away.

But a few minutes later as she watched his plane take off down the runway and soar into the skies towards the east, the maiden schoolteacher made up her mind that some of his feeling was for her, personally, as a woman. And she drove home without touching the pavements.